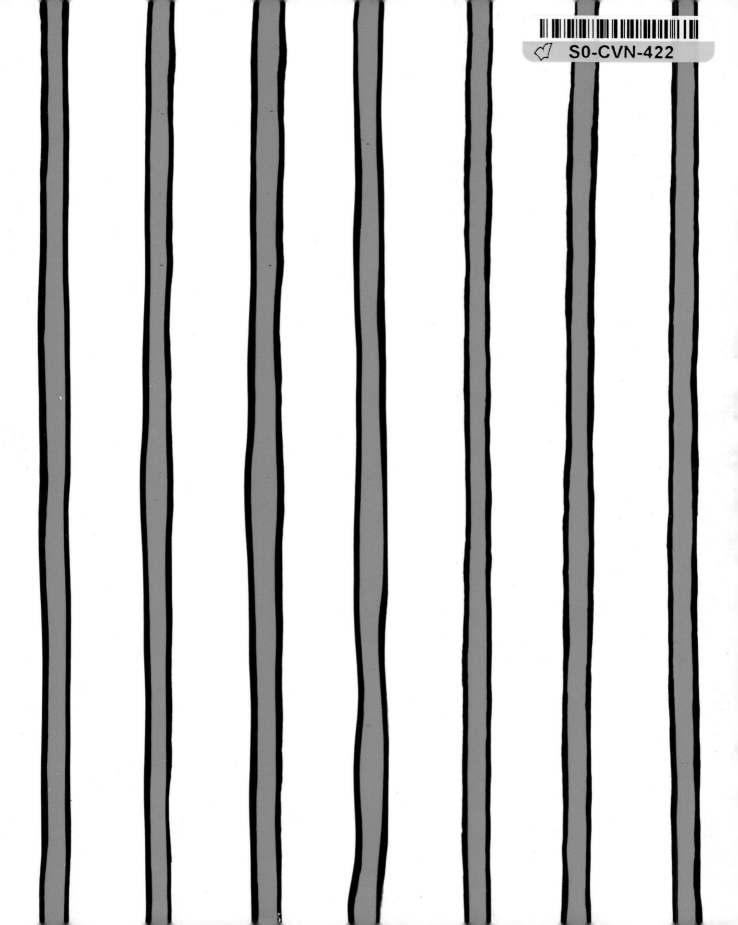

S0-CVN-422

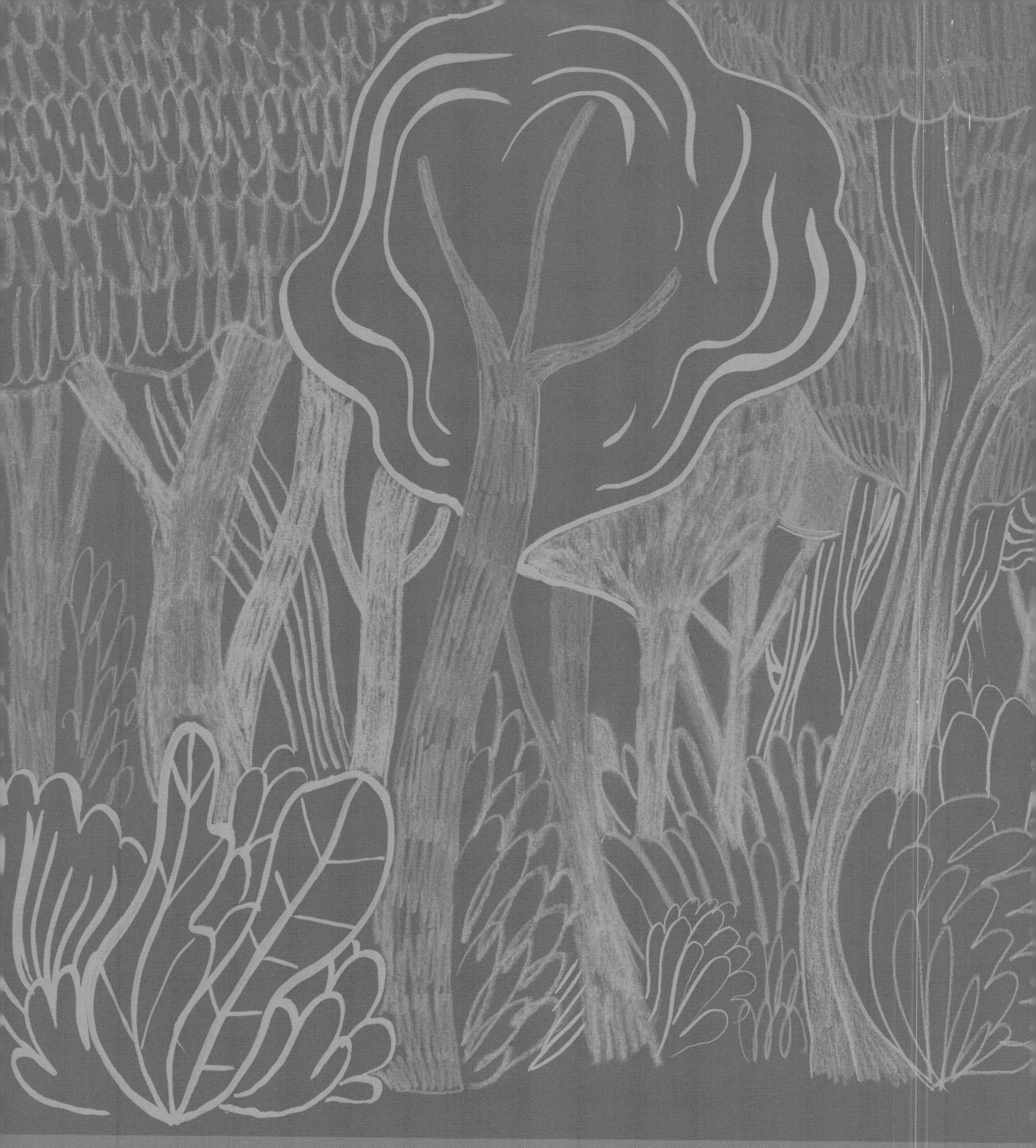

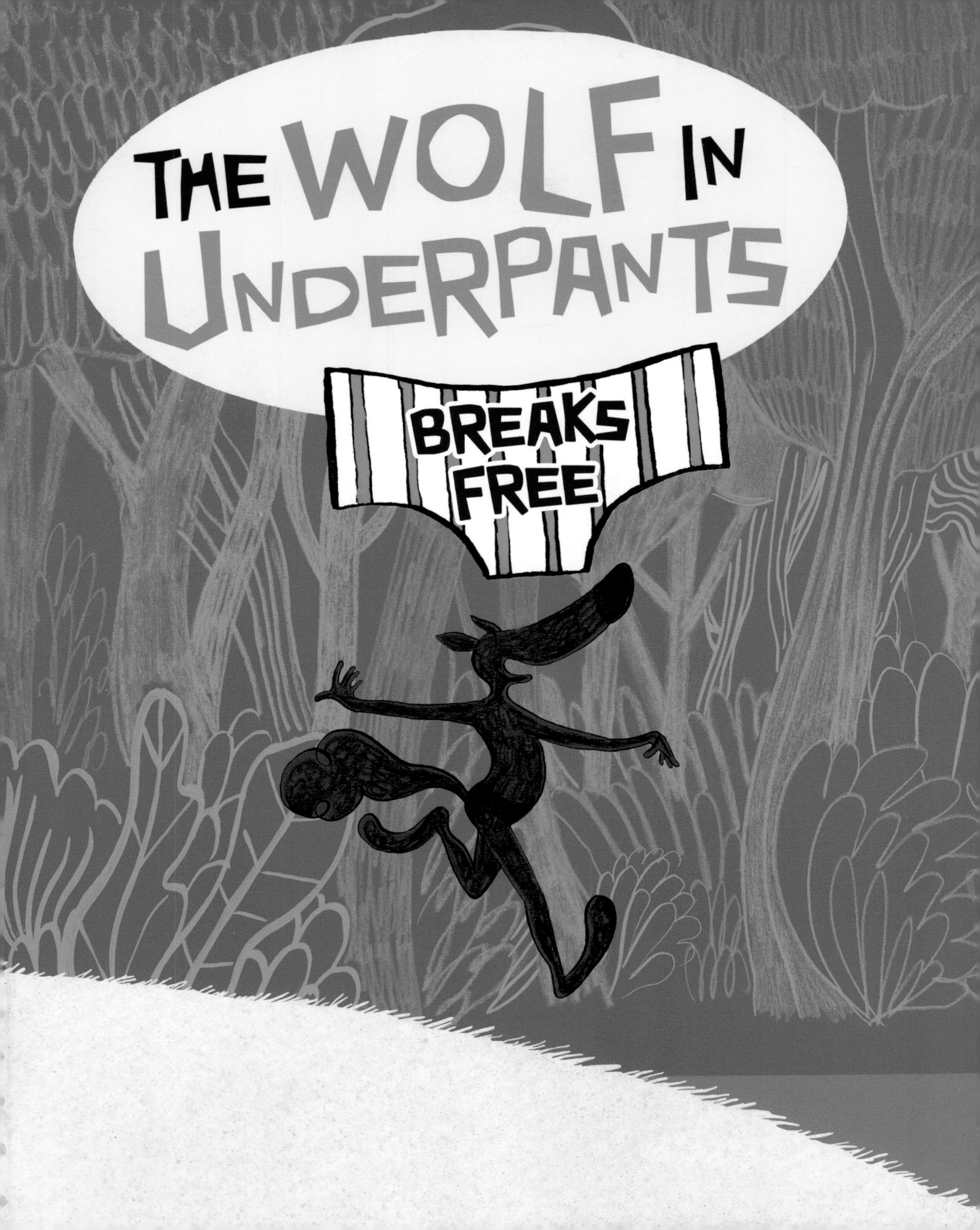
THE WOLF IN
UNDERPANTS
BREAKS
FREE

Story by Wilfrid Lupano
Art by Mayana Itoïz
With the friendly artistic participation of Paul Cauuet
Translation by Nathan Sacks

First American edition published in 2022 by Graphic Universe™
Published by arrangement with Mediatoon Licensing - France
Le Loup en slip n'en fiche pas une
© Dargaud Benelux (Dargaud-Lombard S.A.) 2019—Lupano, Itoïz, and Cauuet. All rights
reserved. Original artistic director: Philippe Ravon.
www.dargaud.com

Graphic Universe™
An imprint of Lerner Publishing Group, Inc.
241 First Avenue North
Minneapolis, MN 55401 USA

For reading levels and more information, look up this title at www.lernerbooks.com.

Main body text set in Stick-A-Round. Typeface provided by Pintassilgoprints.

Library of Congress Cataloging-in-Publication Data

Names: Lupano, Wilfrid, 1971- author. | Itoïz, Mayana, 1978- artist. | Cauuet, Paul, 1980-
    artist. | Sacks, Nathan, translator.
Title: The wolf in underpants breaks free / story by Wilfrid Lupano ; art by Mayana Itoïz ;
    with the friendly artistic participation of Paul Cauuet ; translation by Nathan Sacks.
Other titles: Loup en slip n'en fiche pas une. English
Description: First American edition. | Minneapolis : Graphic Universe, 2022. | Series: The wolf
    in underpants | Audience: Ages 7–11 | Audience: Grades 2–3 | Summary: "The Wolf helps
    out around the forest but does not ask for coins in return. Some other animals get
    suspicious—and toss the Wolf in prison!"— Provided by publisher.
Identifiers: LCCN 2021053100 (print) | LCCN 2021053101 (ebook) | ISBN 9781728459004
    (library binding) | ISBN 9781728462967 (paperback) | ISBN 9781728461021 (ebook)
Subjects: CYAC: Graphic novels. | Wolves—Fiction. | Forest animals—Fiction. | LCGFT: Funny
    animal comics. | Graphic novels.
Classification: LCC PZ7.7.L86 Wpf 2022 (print) | LCC PZ7.7.L86 (ebook) | DDC 741.5/973—
    dc23/eng/20211116

LC record available at https://lccn.loc.gov/2021053100
LC ebook record available at https://lccn.loc.gov/2021053101

Manufactured in the United States of America
1-50976-50239-2/16/2022

THE WOLF IN UNDERPANTS BREAKS FREE

Wilfrid Lupano

Mayana Itoïz
and
Paul Cauuet

Graphic Universe™ • Minneapolis

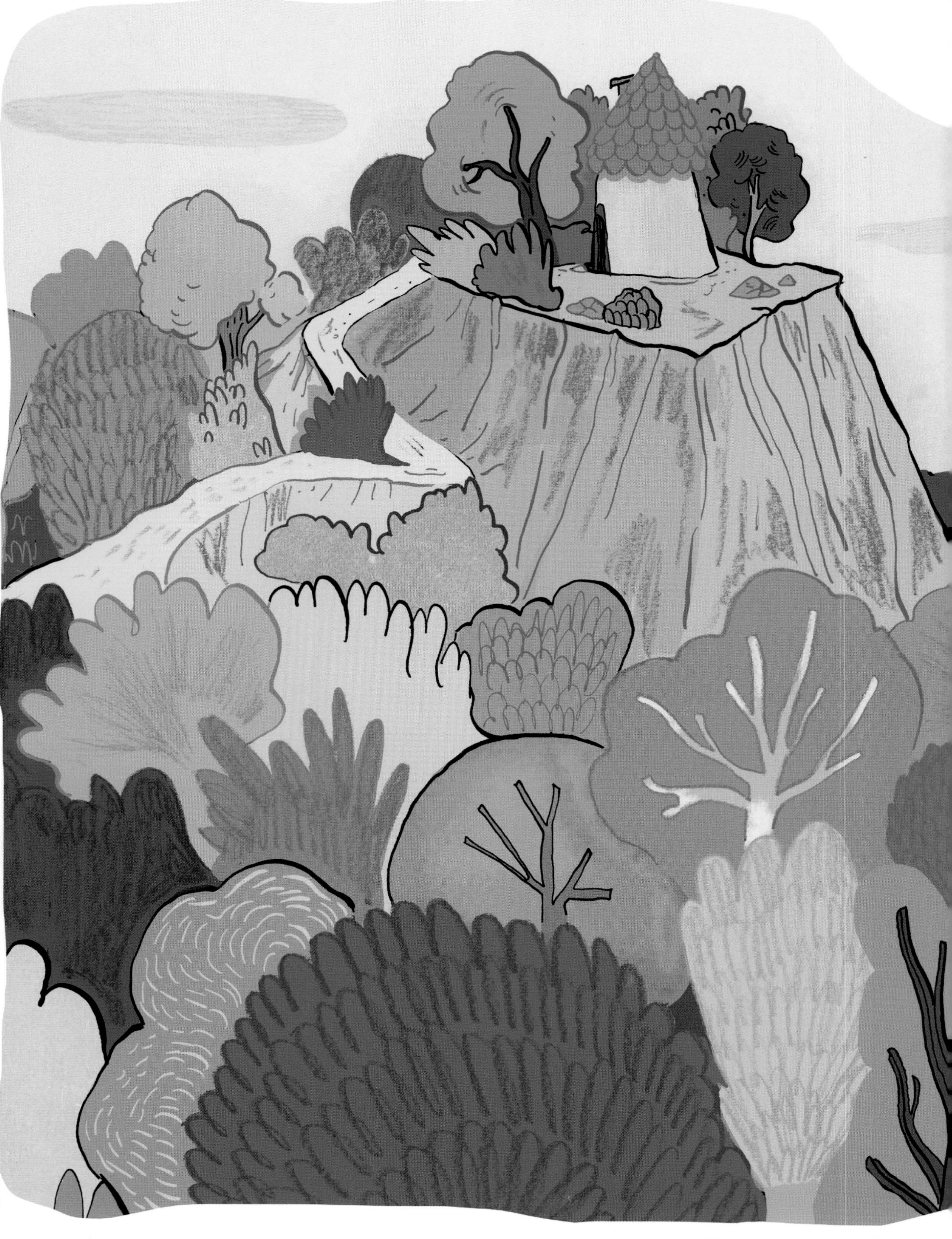

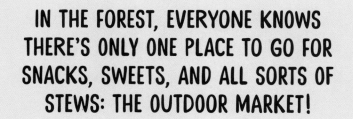

IN THE FOREST, EVERYONE KNOWS
THERE'S ONLY ONE PLACE TO GO FOR
SNACKS, SWEETS, AND ALL SORTS OF
STEWS: THE OUTDOOR MARKET!

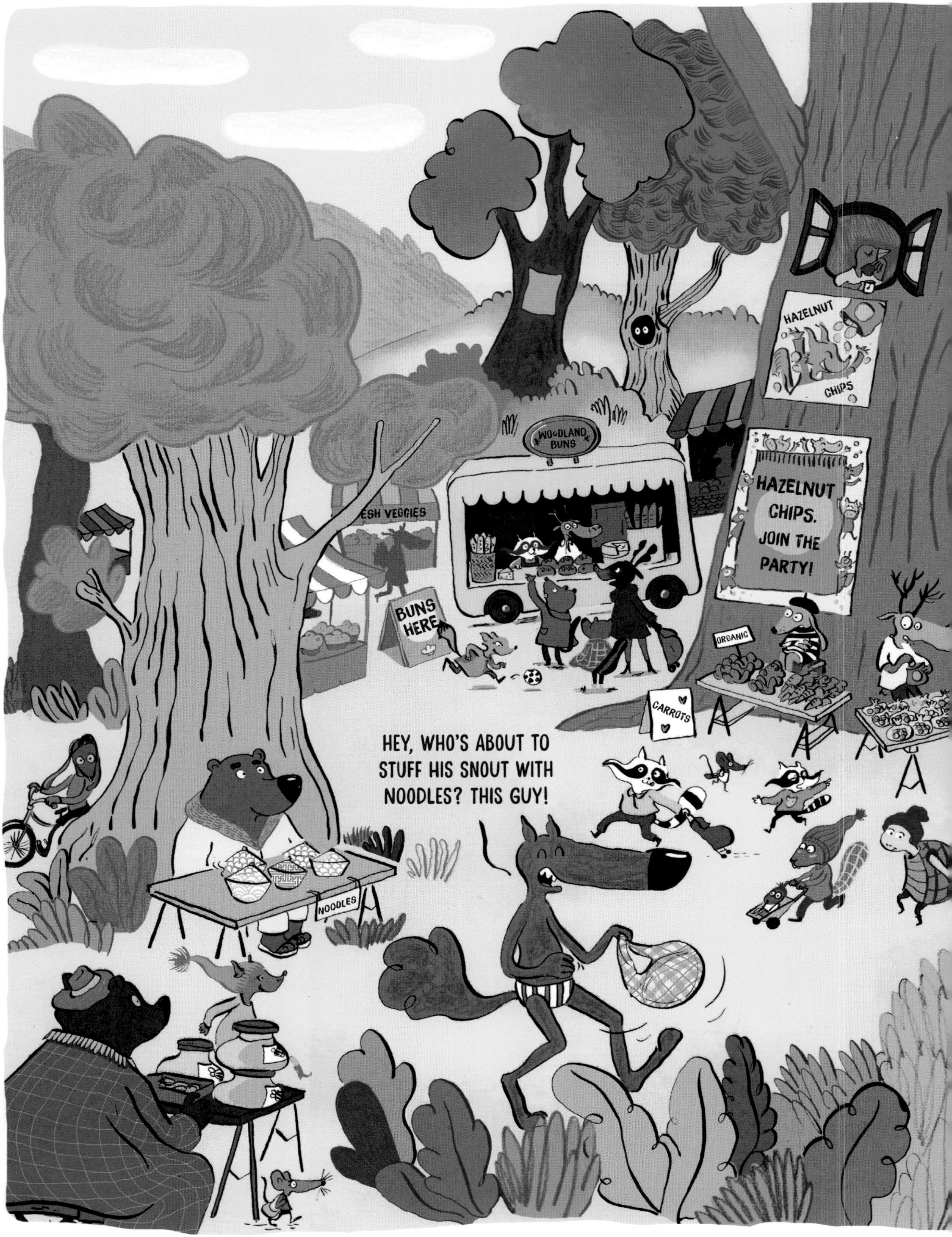
WOODLAND BUNS
ESH VEGGIES
BUNS HERE
HAZELNUT
CHIPS
HAZELNUT CHIPS. JOIN THE PARTY!
ORGANIC
CARROTS
HEY, WHO'S ABOUT TO STUFF HIS SNOUT WITH NOODLES? THIS GUY!
NOODLES

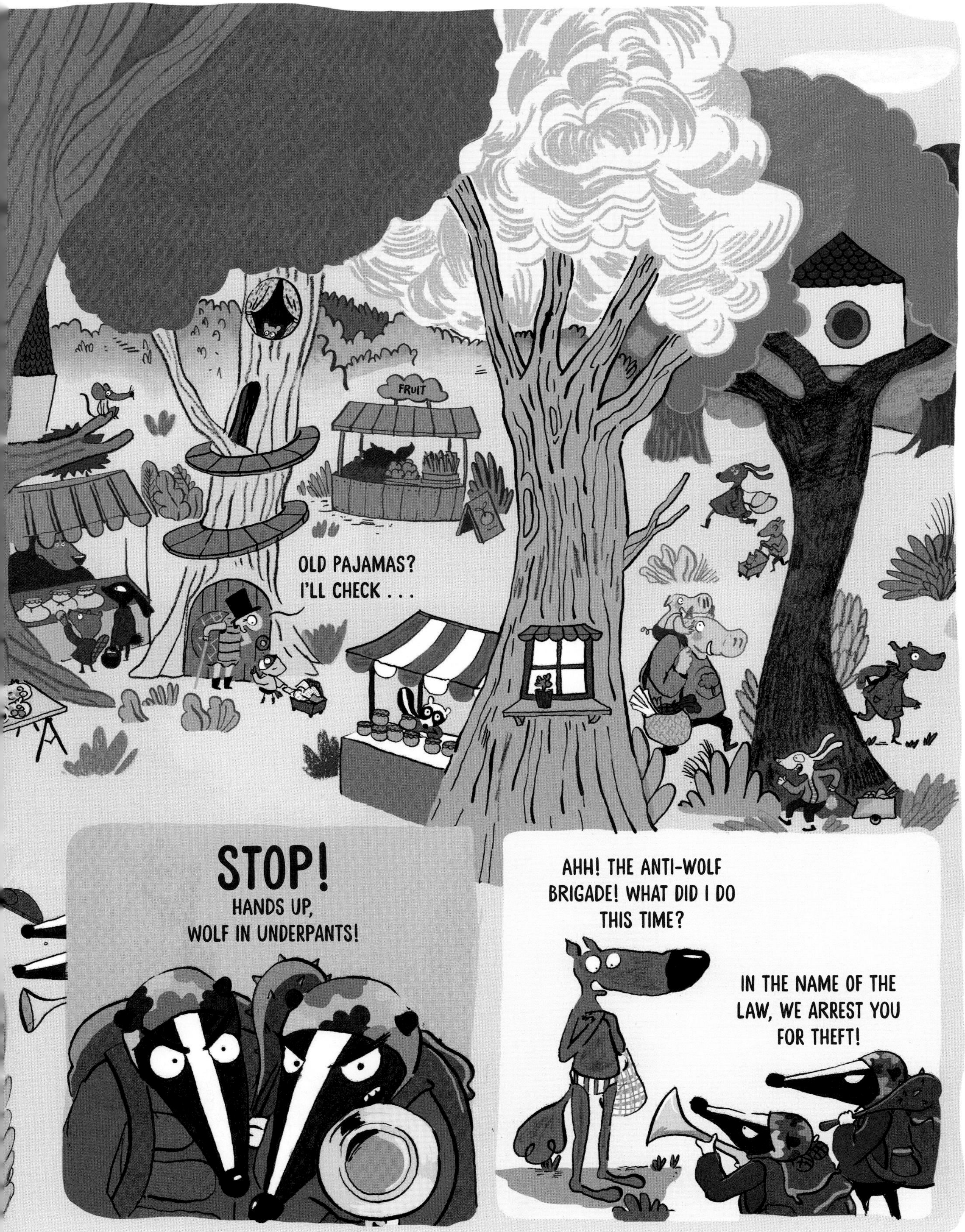
FRUIT
OLD PAJAMAS? I'LL CHECK . . .
STOP! HANDS UP, WOLF IN UNDERPANTS!
AHH! THE ANTI-WOLF BRIGADE! WHAT DID I DO THIS TIME?
IN THE NAME OF THE LAW, WE ARREST YOU FOR THEFT!

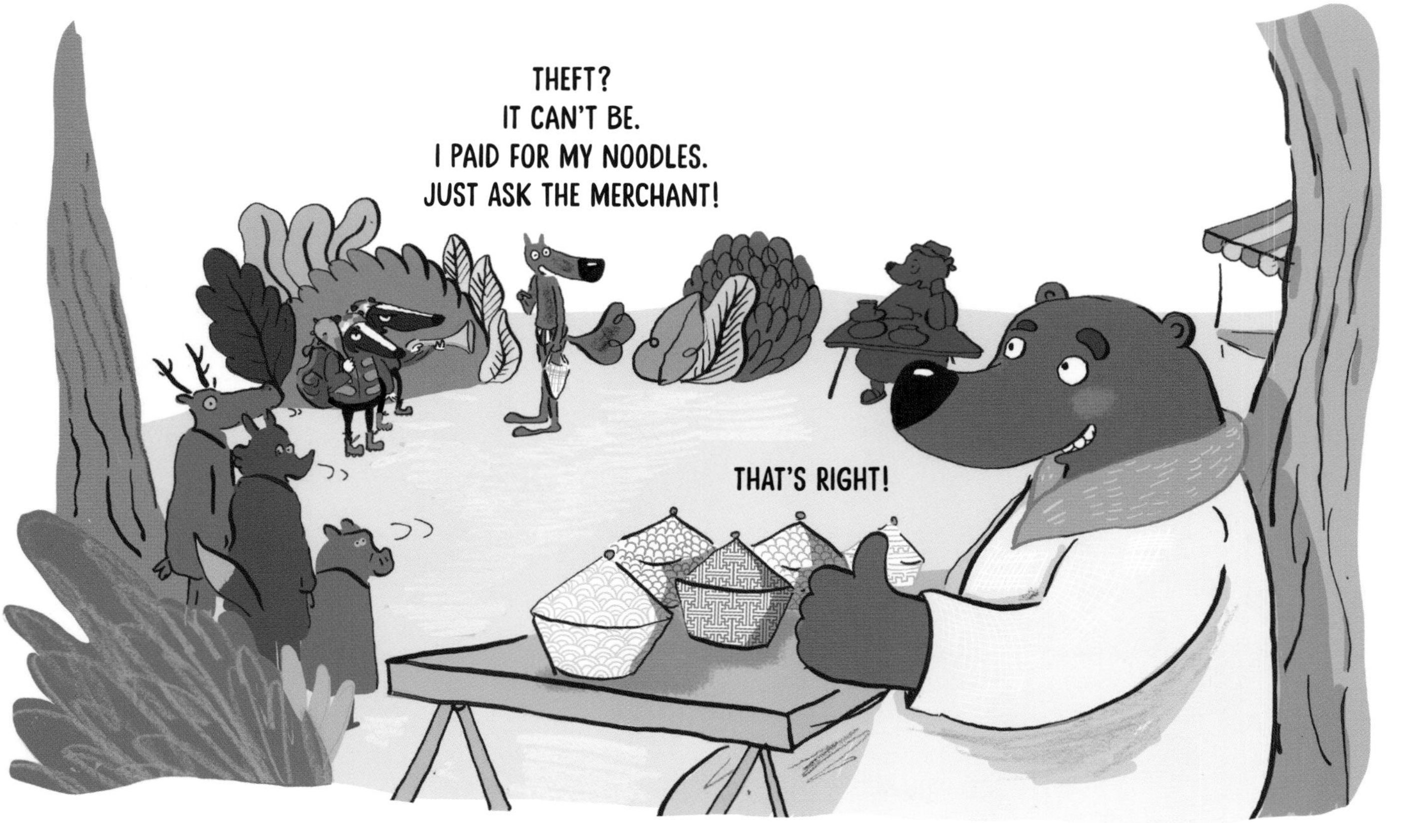
THEFT?
IT CAN'T BE.
I PAID FOR MY NOODLES.
JUST ASK THE MERCHANT!
THAT'S RIGHT!

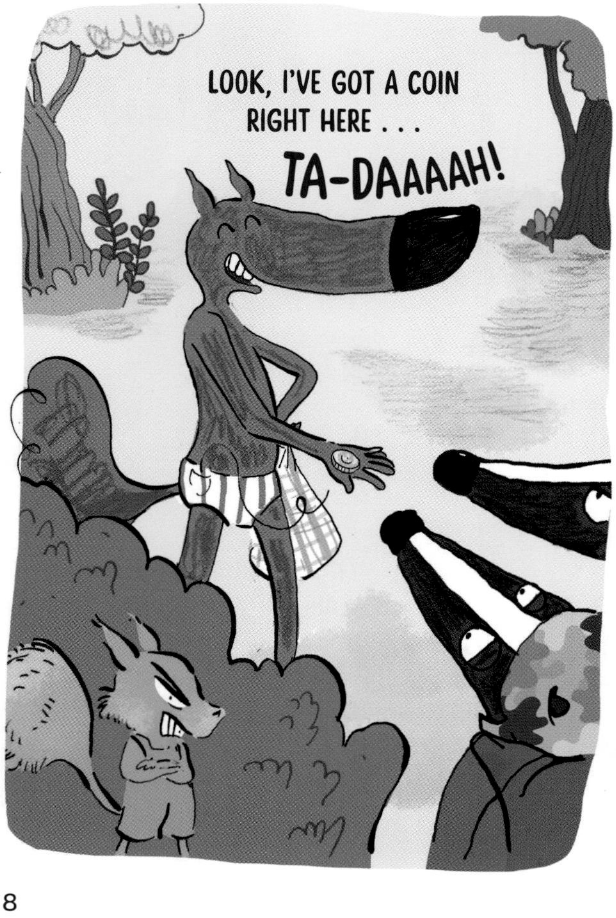
LOOK, I'VE GOT A COIN
RIGHT HERE . . .
TA-DAAAAH!

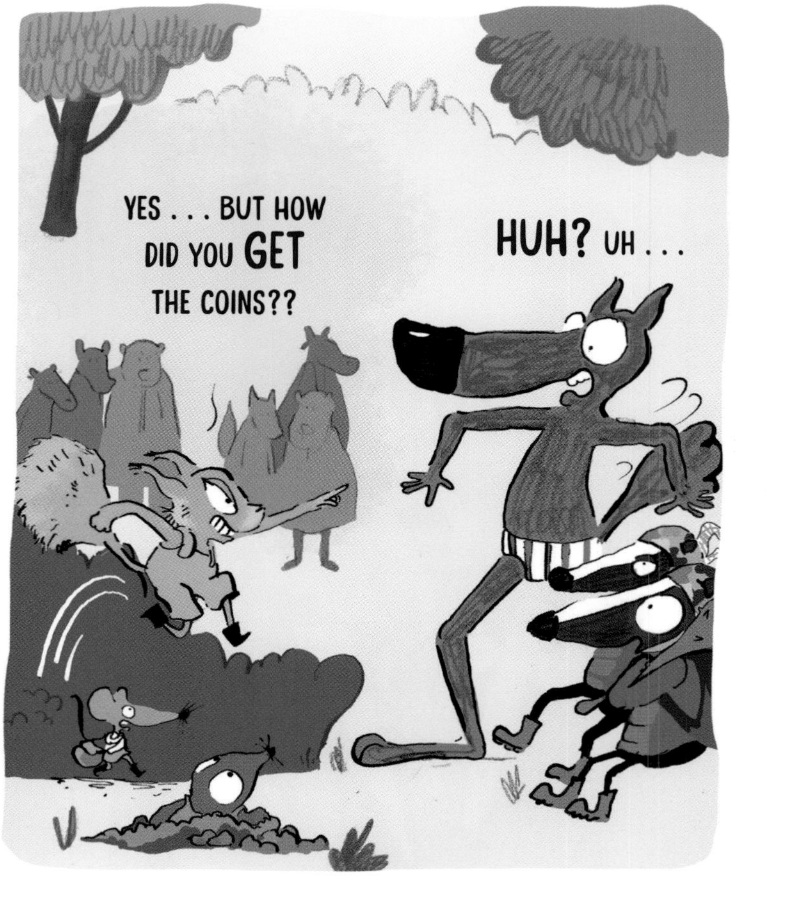
YES . . . BUT HOW
DID YOU GET
THE COINS??
HUH? UH . . .

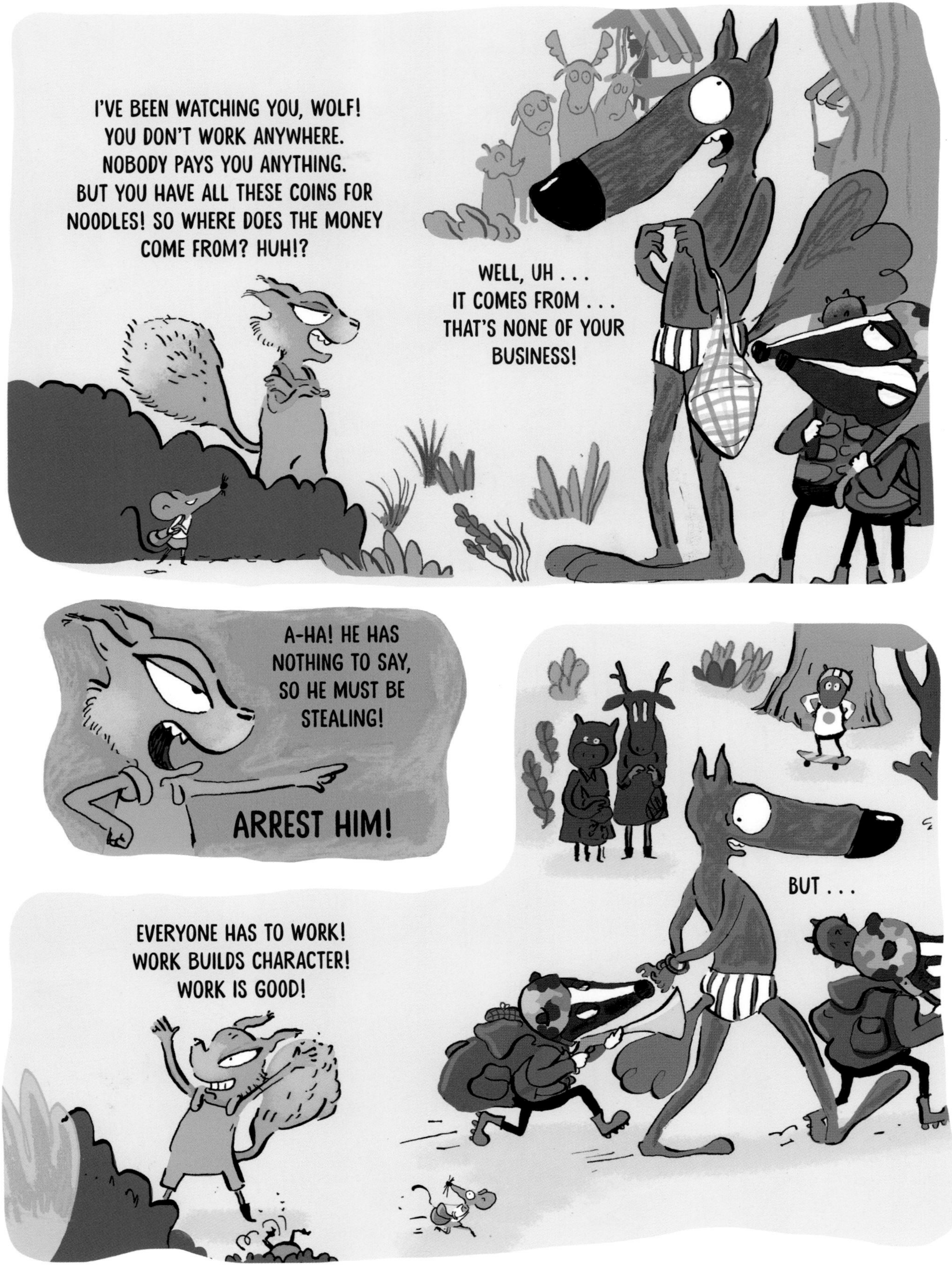
I'VE BEEN WATCHING YOU, WOLF! YOU DON'T WORK ANYWHERE. NOBODY PAYS YOU ANYTHING. BUT YOU HAVE ALL THESE COINS FOR NOODLES! SO WHERE DOES THE MONEY COME FROM? HUH!?
WELL, UH . . . IT COMES FROM . . . THAT'S NONE OF YOUR BUSINESS!
A-HA! HE HAS NOTHING TO SAY, SO HE MUST BE STEALING!
ARREST HIM!
BUT . . .
EVERYONE HAS TO WORK! WORK BUILDS CHARACTER! WORK IS GOOD!

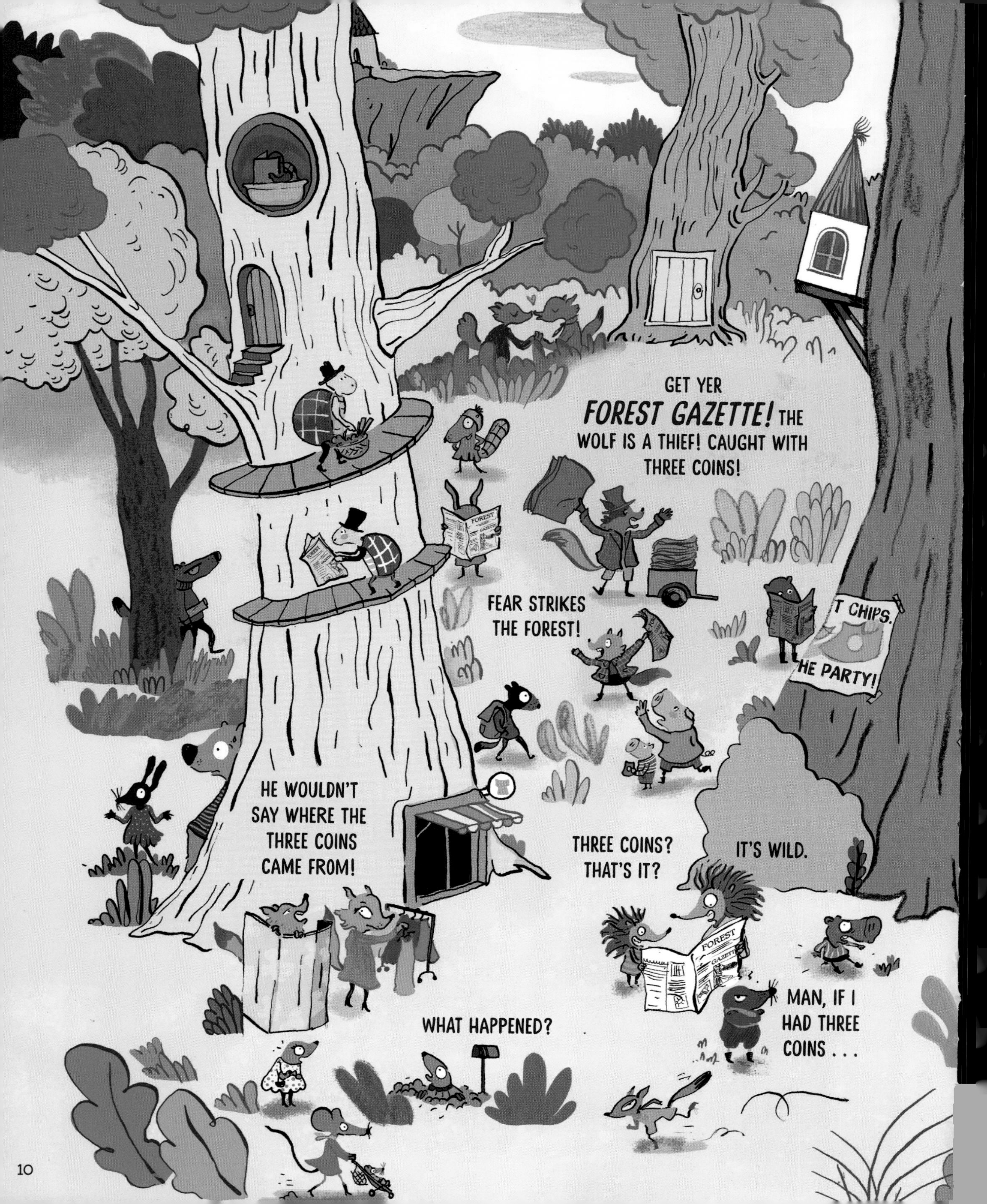
GET YER FORREST GAZETTE! THE WOLF IS A THIEF! CAUGHT WITH THREE COINS!
FEAR STRIKES THE FOREST!
T CHIPS.
HE PARTY!
HE WOULDN'T SAY WHERE THE THREE COINS CAME FROM!
THREE COINS? THAT'S IT?
IT'S WILD.
WHAT HAPPENED?
MAN, IF I HAD THREE COINS . . .

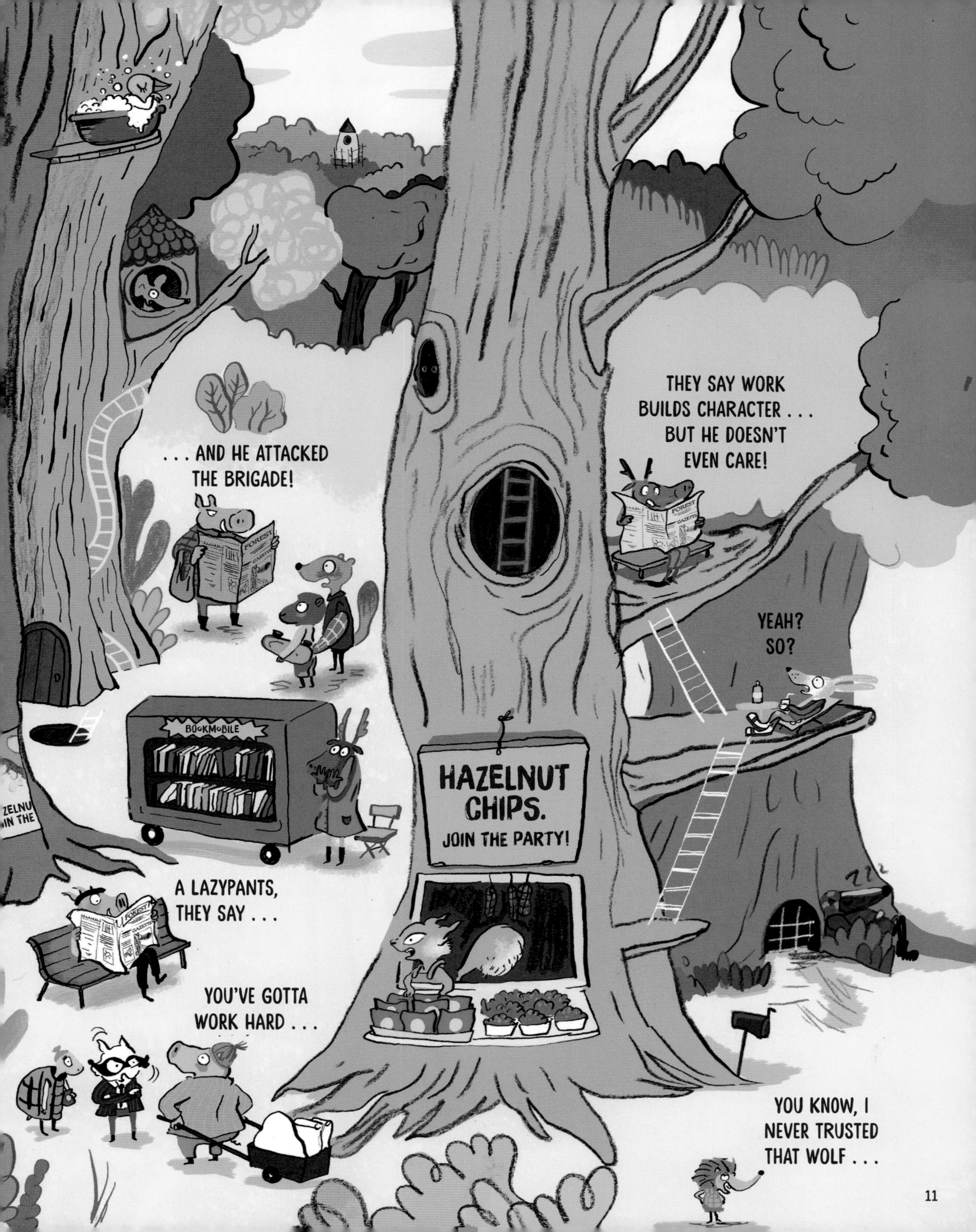
. . . AND HE ATTACKED THE BRIGADE!
THEY SAY WORK BUILDS CHARACTER . . . BUT HE DOESN'T EVEN CARE!
YEAH? SO?
BOOKMOBILE
HAZELNUT CHIPS.
JOIN THE PARTY!
A LAZYPANTS, THEY SAY . . .
YOU'VE GOTTA WORK HARD . . .
YOU KNOW, I NEVER TRUSTED THAT WOLF . . .

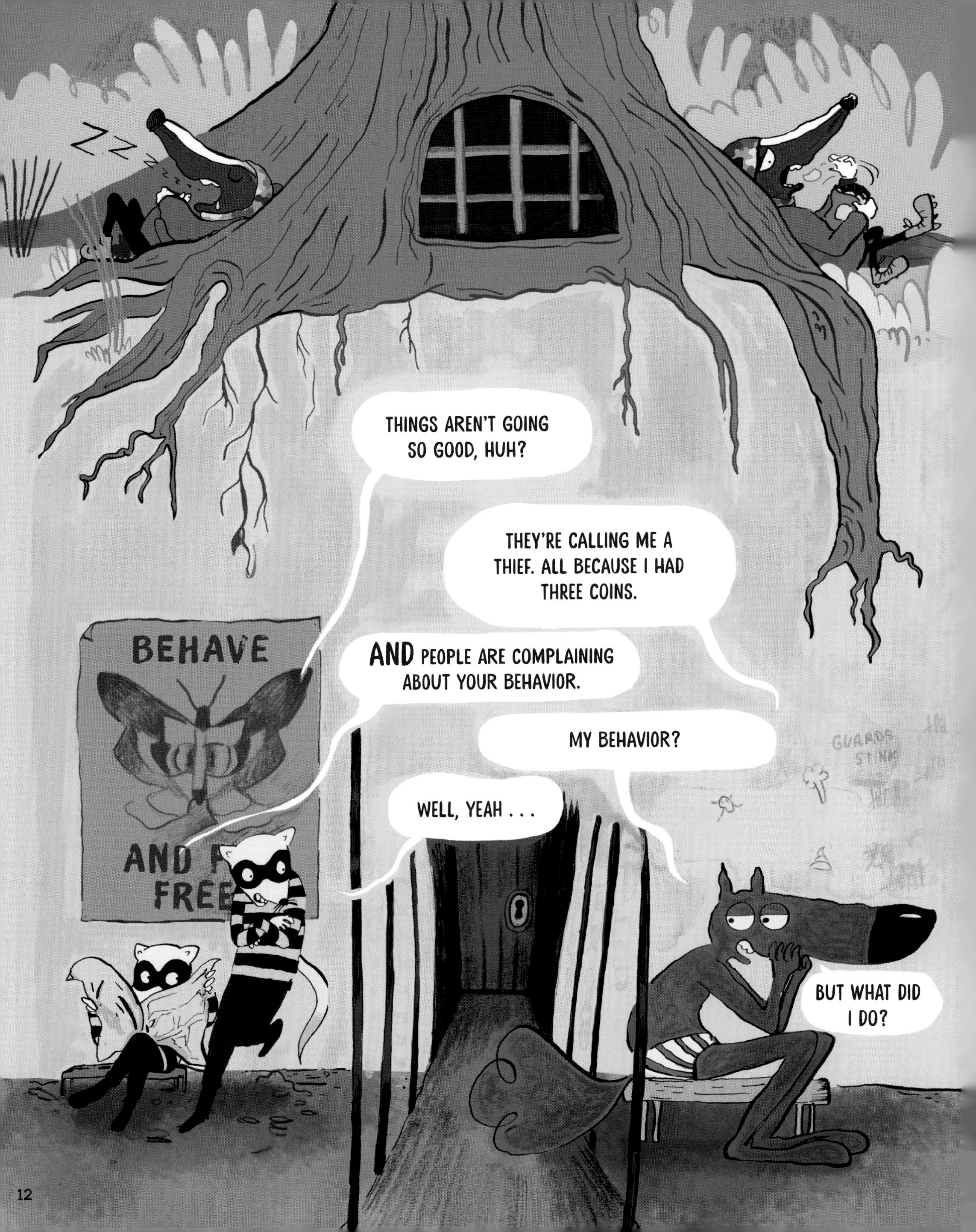
Z Z Z
THINGS AREN'T GOING SO GOOD, HUH?
THEY'RE CALLING ME A THIEF. ALL BECAUSE I HAD THREE COINS.
AND PEOPLE ARE COMPLAINING ABOUT YOUR BEHAVIOR.
MY BEHAVIOR?
WELL, YEAH . . .
BUT WHAT DID I DO?
BEHAVE
AND
FREE
GUARDS STINK

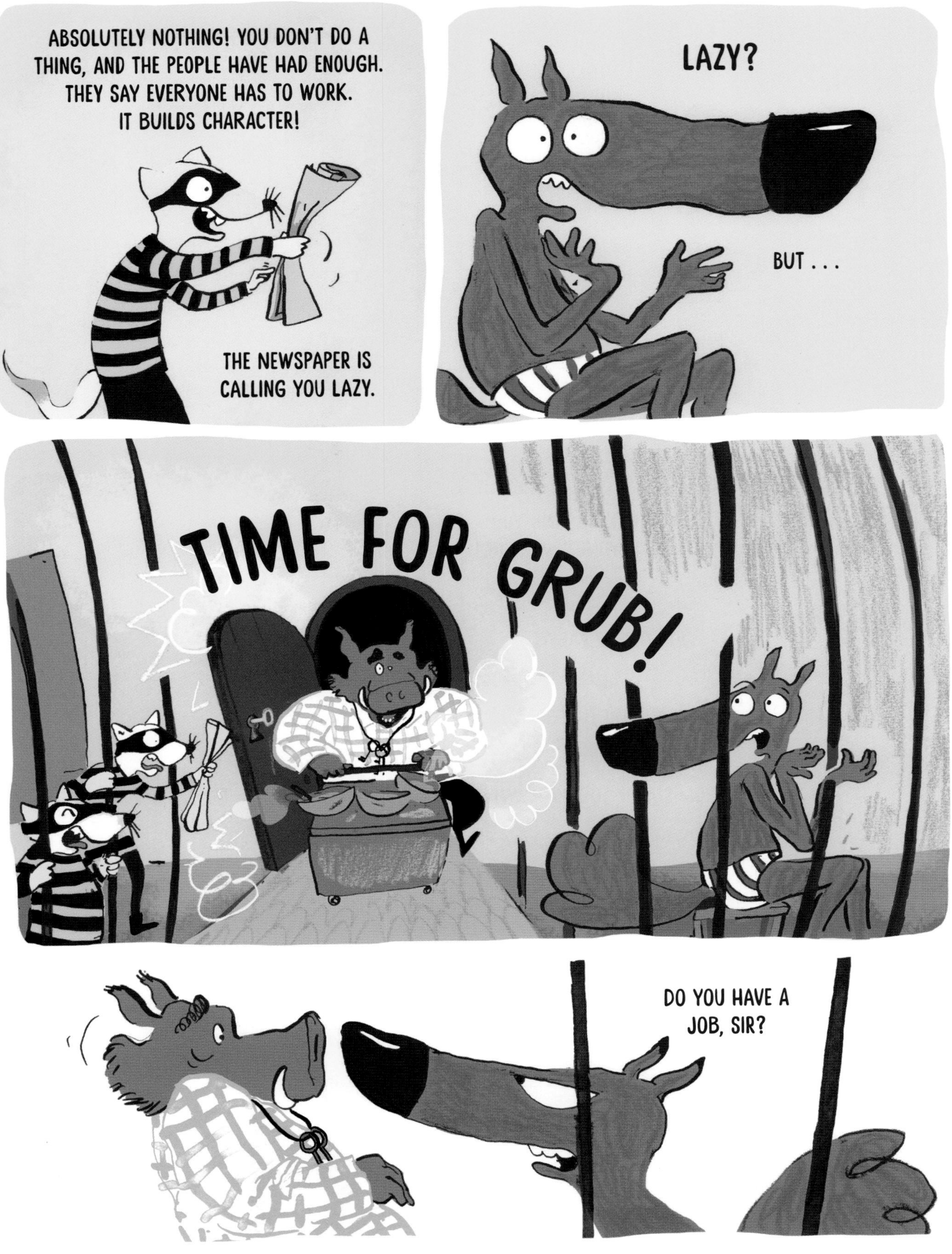
ABSOLUTELY NOTHING! YOU DON'T DO A THING, AND THE PEOPLE HAVE HAD ENOUGH. THEY SAY EVERYONE HAS TO WORK. IT BUILDS CHARACTER!
THE NEWSPAPER IS CALLING YOU LAZY.
LAZY?
BUT . . .
TIME FOR GRUB!
DO YOU HAVE A JOB, SIR?

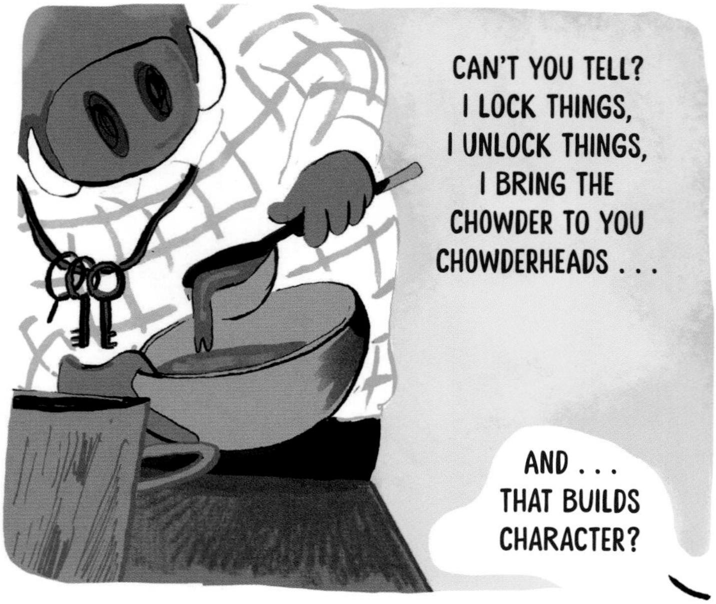
CAN'T YOU TELL? I LOCK THINGS, I UNLOCK THINGS, I BRING THE CHOWDER TO YOU CHOWDERHEADS . . .
AND . . . THAT BUILDS CHARACTER?

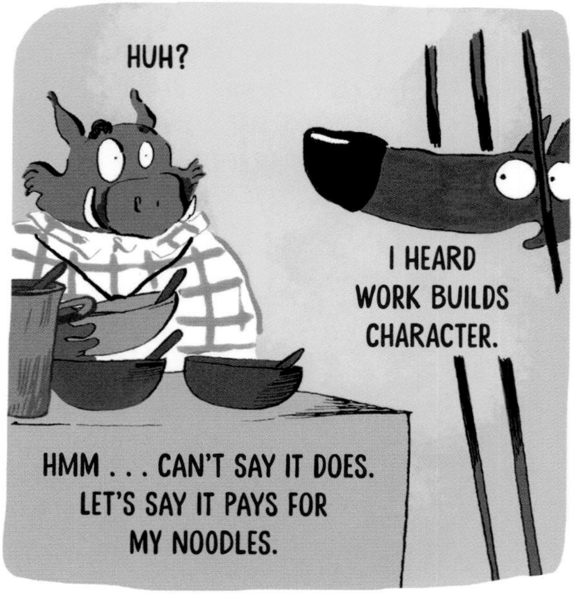
HUH?
I HEARD WORK BUILDS CHARACTER.
HMM . . . CAN'T SAY IT DOES. LET'S SAY IT PAYS FOR MY NOODLES.

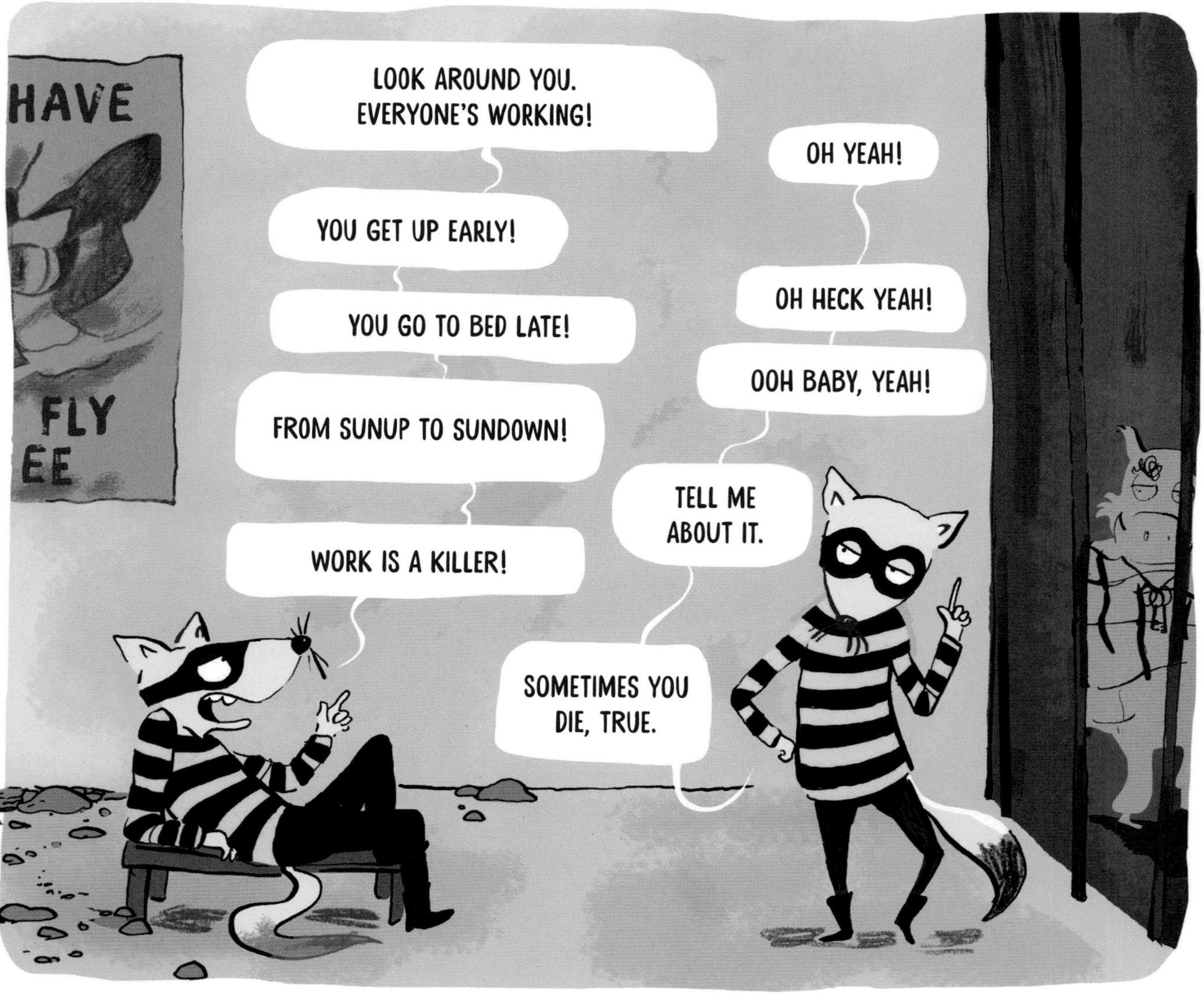
HAVE
FLY
EE
LOOK AROUND YOU. EVERYONE'S WORKING!
OH YEAH!
YOU GET UP EARLY!
OH HECK YEAH!
YOU GO TO BED LATE!
OOH BABY, YEAH!
FROM SUNUP TO SUNDOWN!
TELL ME ABOUT IT.
WORK IS A KILLER!
SOMETIMES YOU DIE, TRUE.

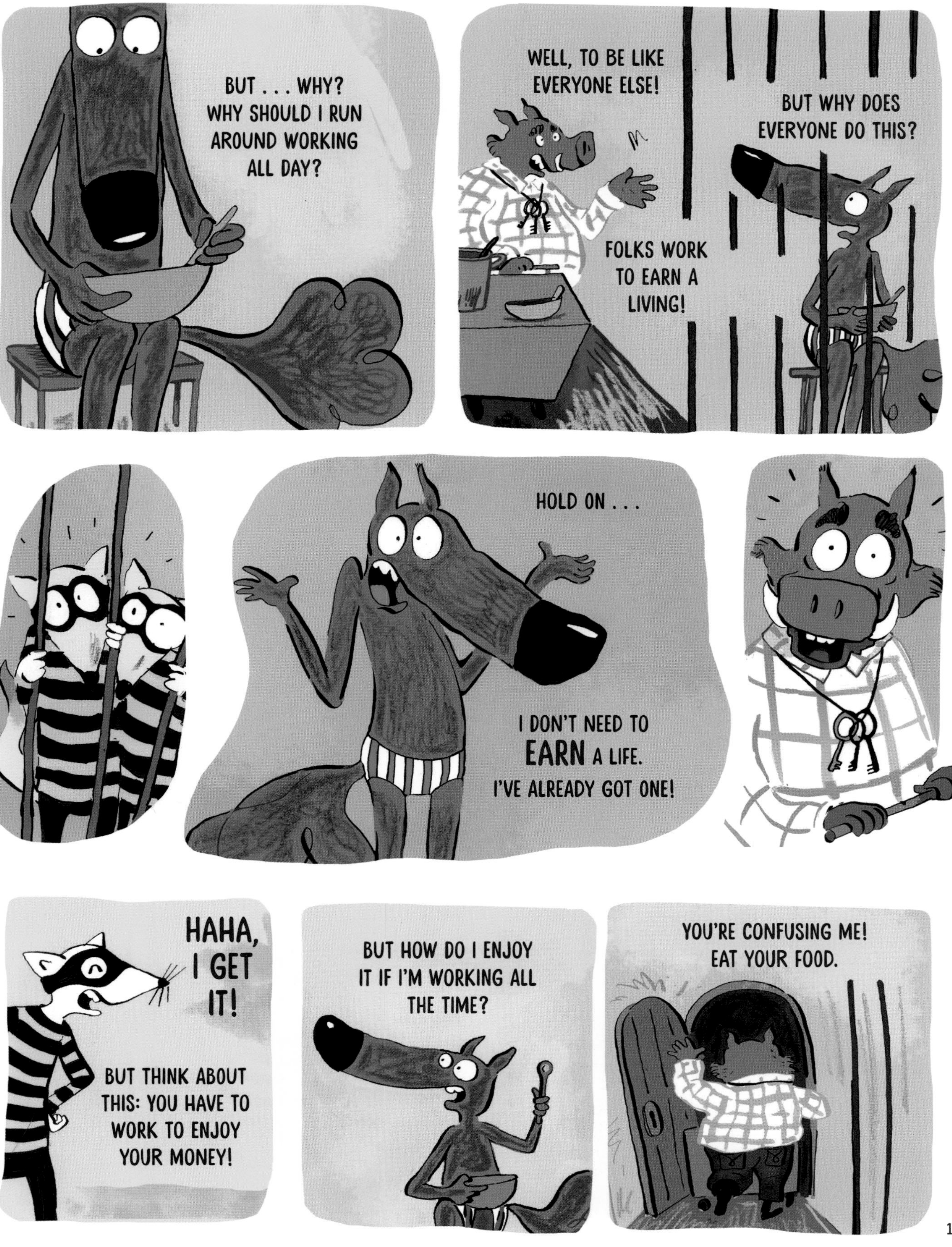
BUT . . . WHY? WHY SHOULD I RUN AROUND WORKING ALL DAY?
WELL, TO BE LIKE EVERYONE ELSE!
FOLKS WORK TO EARN A LIVING!
BUT WHY DOES EVERYONE DO THIS?
HOLD ON . . .
I DON'T NEED TO EARN A LIFE. I'VE ALREADY GOT ONE!
HAHA, I GET IT!
BUT THINK ABOUT THIS: YOU HAVE TO WORK TO ENJOY YOUR MONEY!
BUT HOW DO I ENJOY IT IF I'M WORKING ALL THE TIME?
YOU'RE CONFUSING ME! EAT YOUR FOOD.

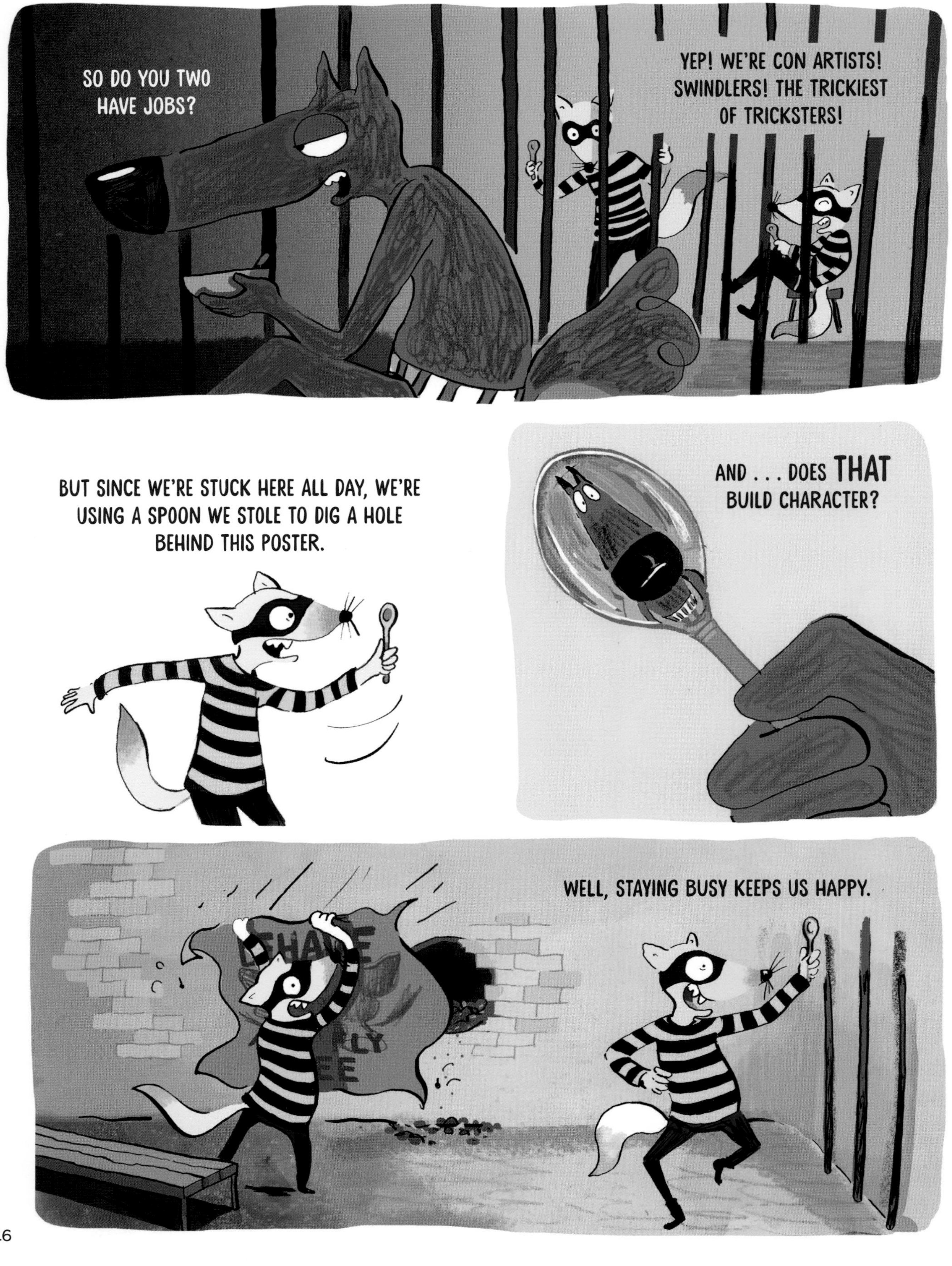
SO DO YOU TWO HAVE JOBS?
YEP! WE'RE CON ARTISTS! SWINDLERS! THE TRICKIEST OF TRICKSTERS!
BUT SINCE WE'RE STUCK HERE ALL DAY, WE'RE USING A SPOON WE STOLE TO DIG A HOLE BEHIND THIS POSTER.
AND . . . DOES THAT BUILD CHARACTER?
WELL, STAYING BUSY KEEPS US HAPPY.

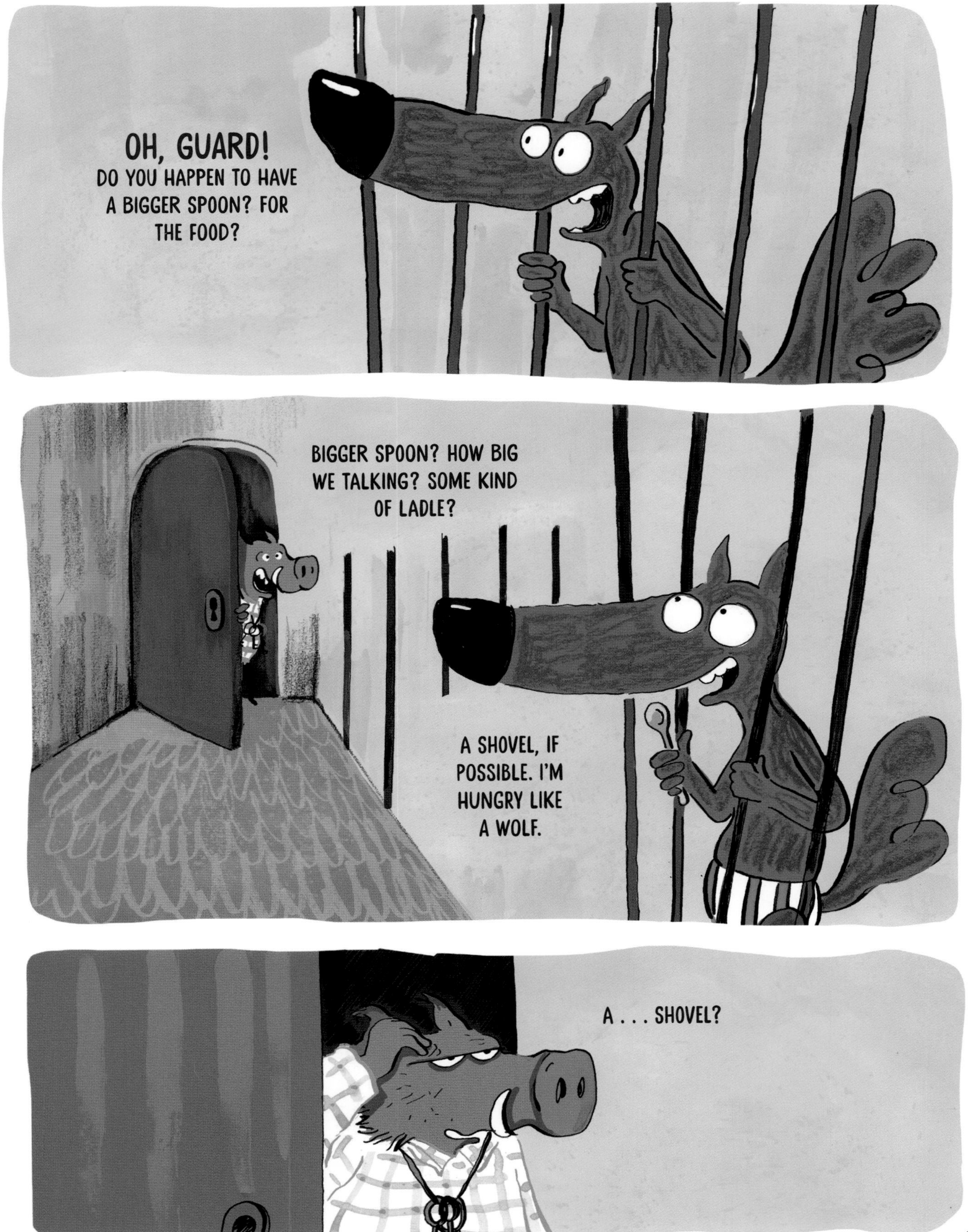

OH, GUARD!
DO YOU HAPPEN TO HAVE A BIGGER SPOON? FOR THE FOOD?
BIGGER SPOON? HOW BIG WE TALKING? SOME KIND OF LADLE?
A SHOVEL, IF POSSIBLE. I'M HUNGRY LIKE A WOLF.
A . . . SHOVEL?

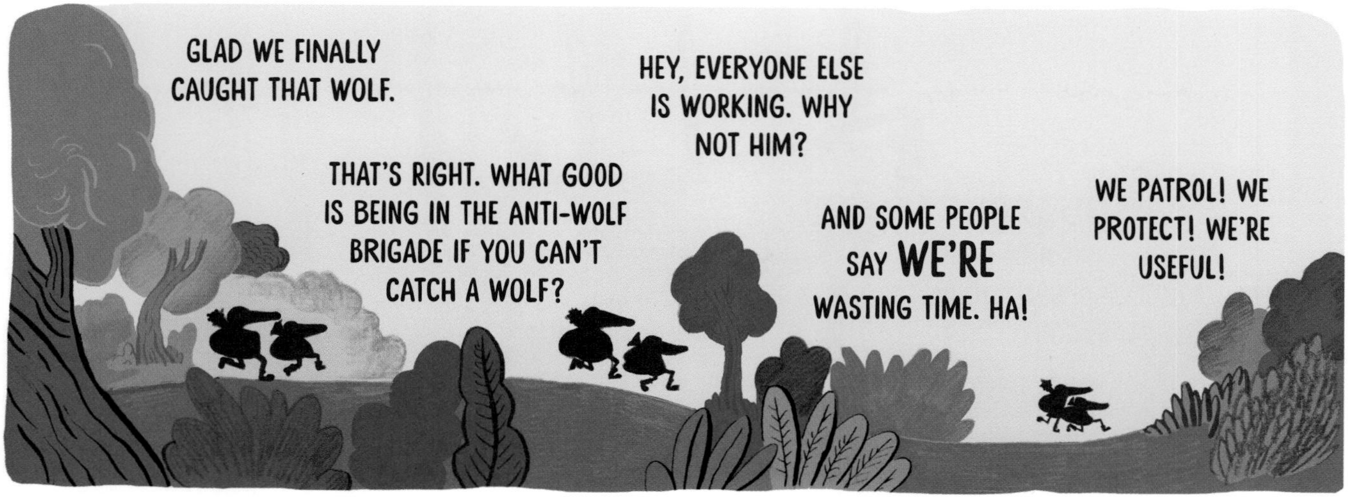

GLAD WE FINALLY CAUGHT THAT WOLF.
THAT'S RIGHT. WHAT GOOD IS BEING IN THE ANTI-WOLF BRIGADE IF YOU CAN'T CATCH A WOLF?
HEY, EVERYONE ELSE IS WORKING. WHY NOT HIM?
AND SOME PEOPLE SAY WE'RE WASTING TIME. HA!
WE PATROL! WE PROTECT! WE'RE USEFUL!

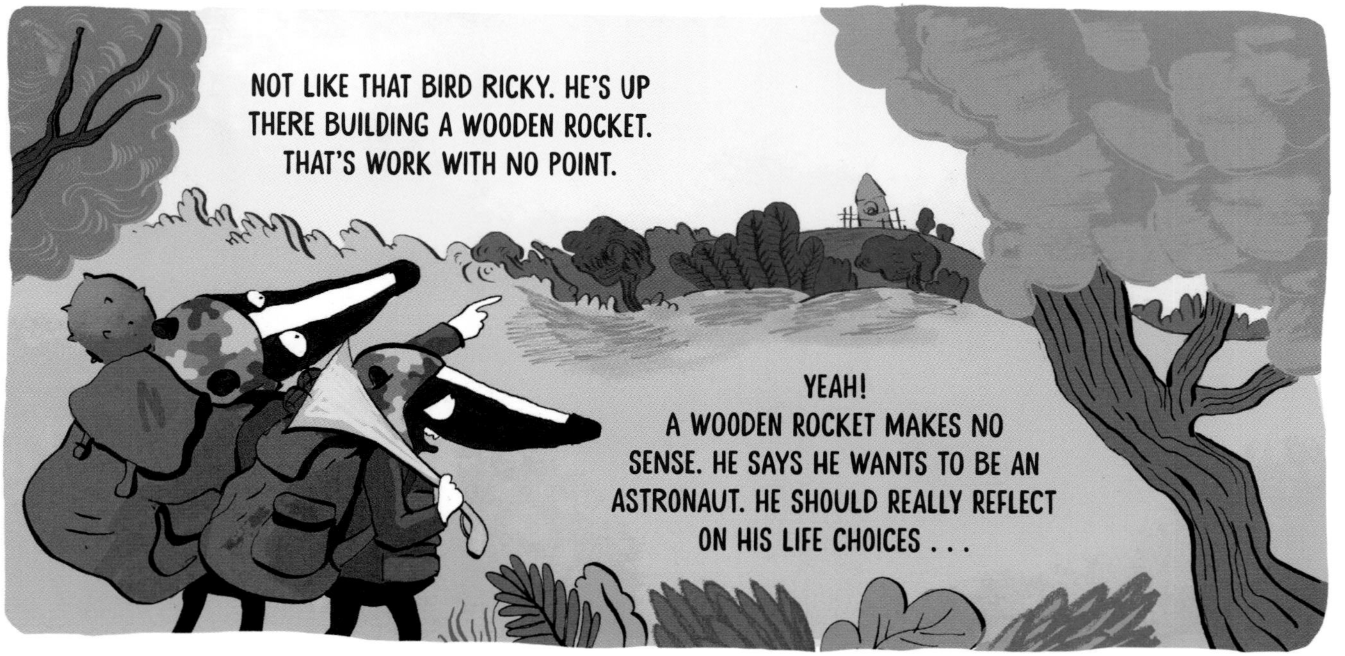

NOT LIKE THAT BIRD RICKY. HE'S UP THERE BUILDING A WOODEN ROCKET. THAT'S WORK WITH NO POINT.
YEAH! A WOODEN ROCKET MAKES NO SENSE. HE SAYS HE WANTS TO BE AN ASTRONAUT. HE SHOULD REALLY REFLECT ON HIS LIFE CHOICES . . .

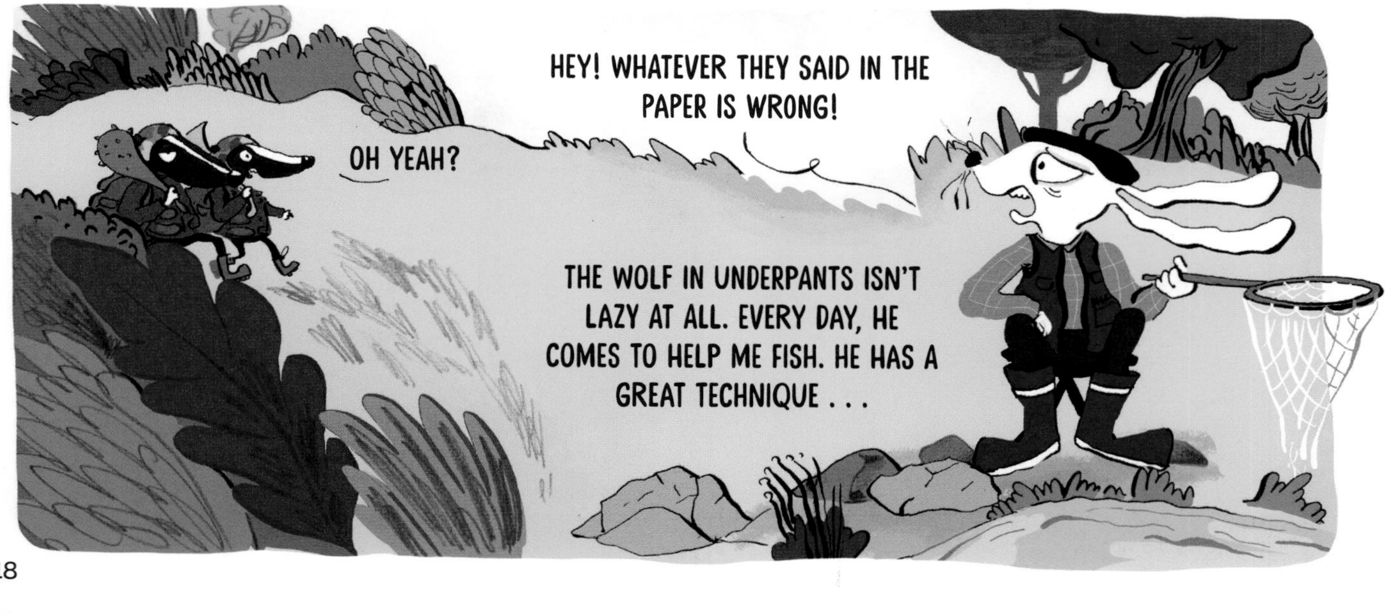

HEY! WHATEVER THEY SAID IN THE PAPER IS WRONG!
OH YEAH?
THE WOLF IN UNDERPANTS ISN'T LAZY AT ALL. EVERY DAY, HE COMES TO HELP ME FISH. HE HAS A GREAT TECHNIQUE . . .

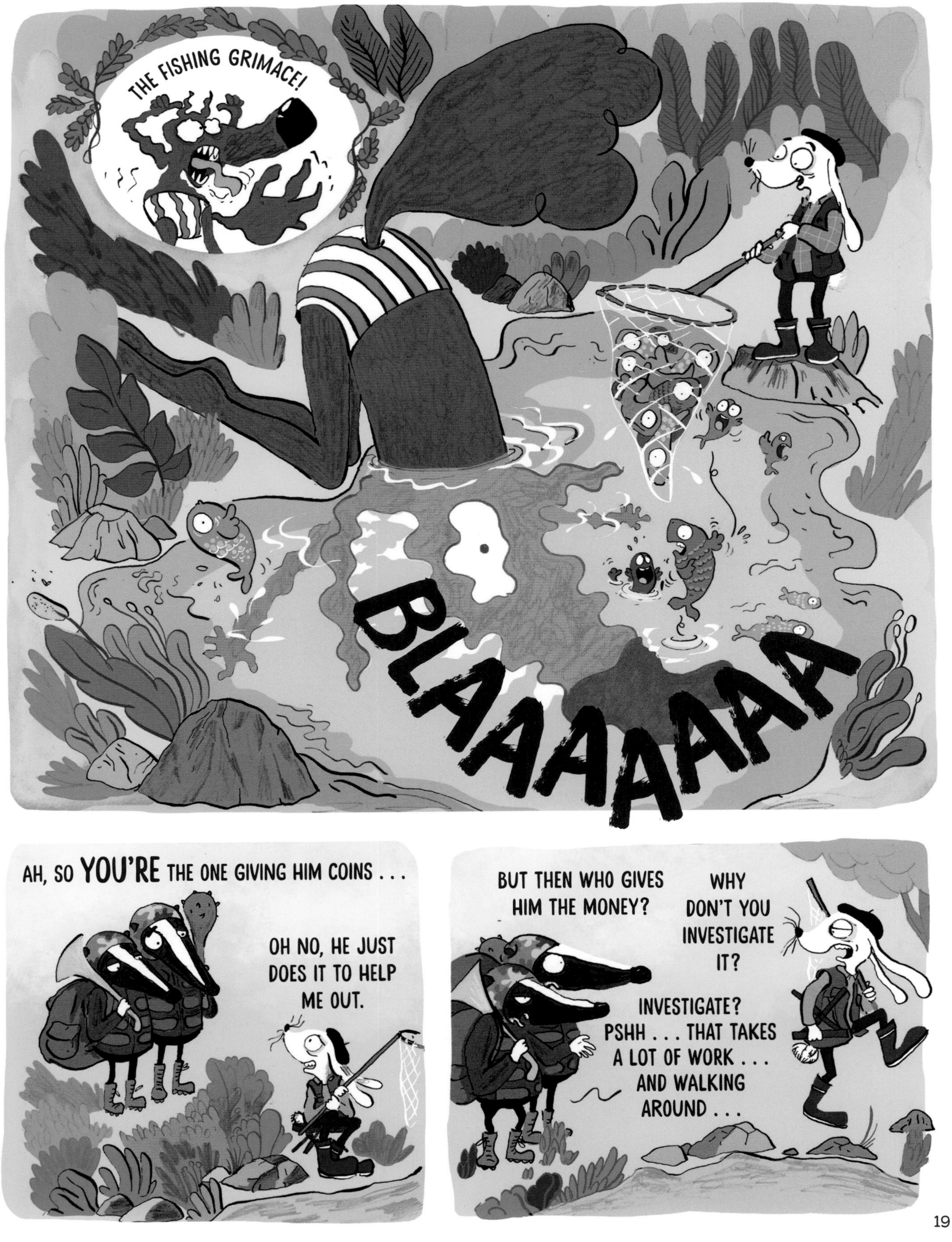
THE FISHING GRIMACE!
BLAAAAAAA
AH, SO YOU'RE THE ONE GIVING HIM COINS . . .
OH NO, HE JUST DOES IT TO HELP ME OUT.
BUT THEN WHO GIVES HIM THE MONEY?
WHY DON'T YOU INVESTIGATE IT?
INVESTIGATE? PSHH . . . THAT TAKES A LOT OF WORK . . . AND WALKING AROUND . . .

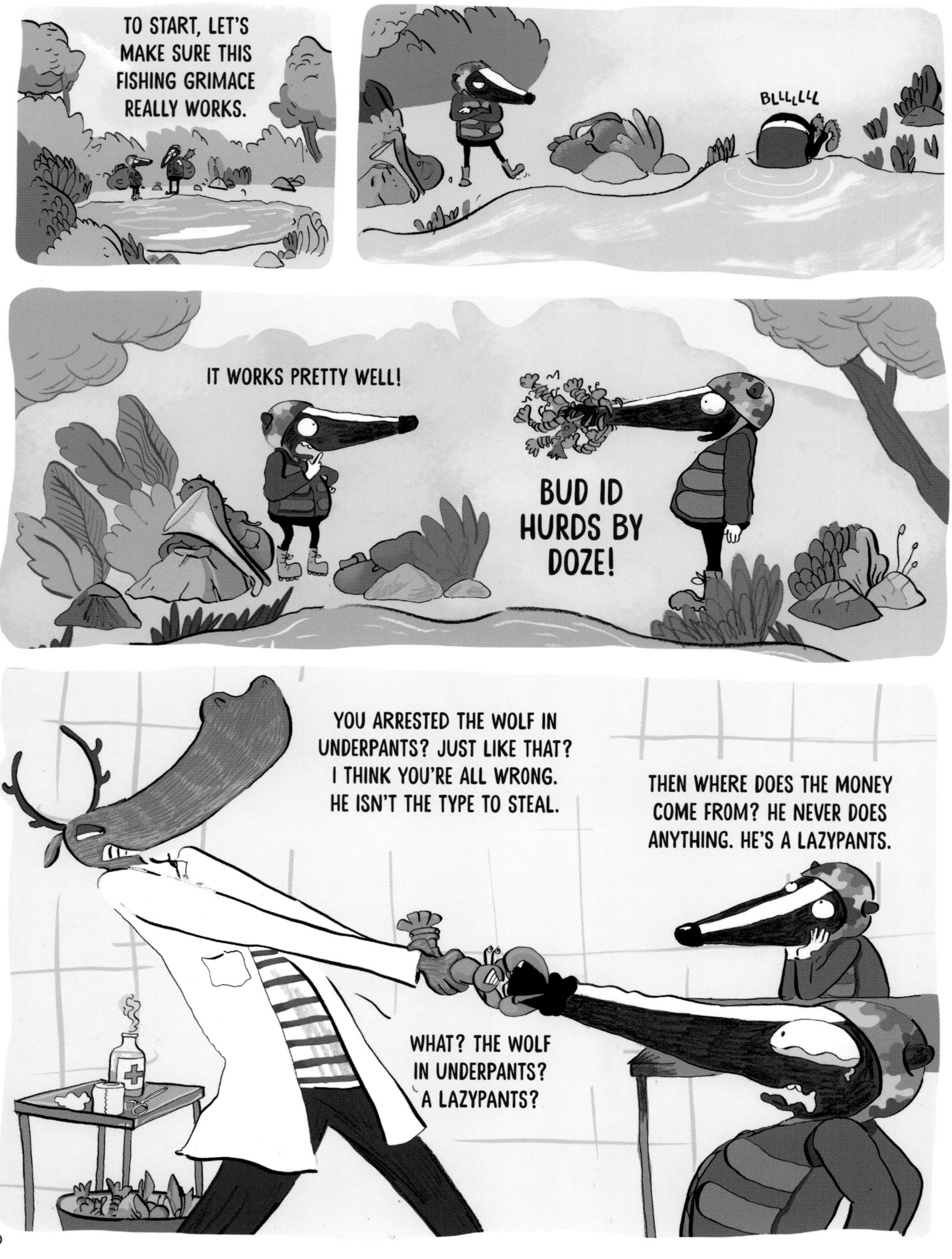
TO START, LET'S MAKE SURE THIS FISHING GRIMACE REALLY WORKS.
BLLLLLLL
IT WORKS PRETTY WELL!
BUD ID HURDS BY DOZE!
YOU ARRESTED THE WOLF IN UNDERPANTS? JUST LIKE THAT? I THINK YOU'RE ALL WRONG. HE ISN'T THE TYPE TO STEAL.
THEN WHERE DOES THE MONEY COME FROM? HE NEVER DOES ANYTHING. HE'S A LAZYPANTS.
WHAT? THE WOLF IN UNDERPANTS? A LAZYPANTS?

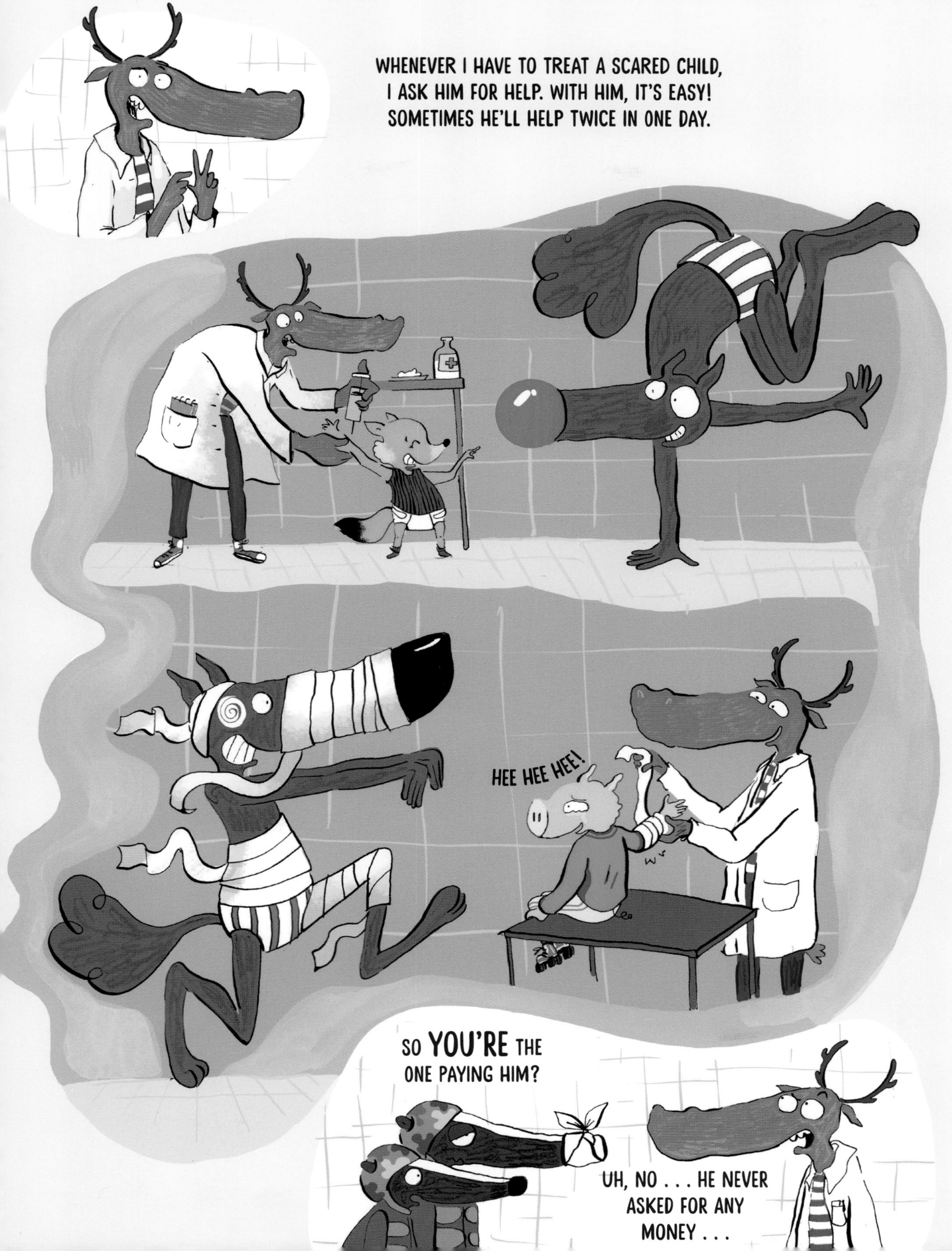

WHENEVER I HAVE TO TREAT A SCARED CHILD, I ASK HIM FOR HELP. WITH HIM, IT'S EASY! SOMETIMES HE'LL HELP TWICE IN ONE DAY.
HEE HEE HEE!
SO YOU'RE THE ONE PAYING HIM?
UH, NO . . . HE NEVER ASKED FOR ANY MONEY . . .

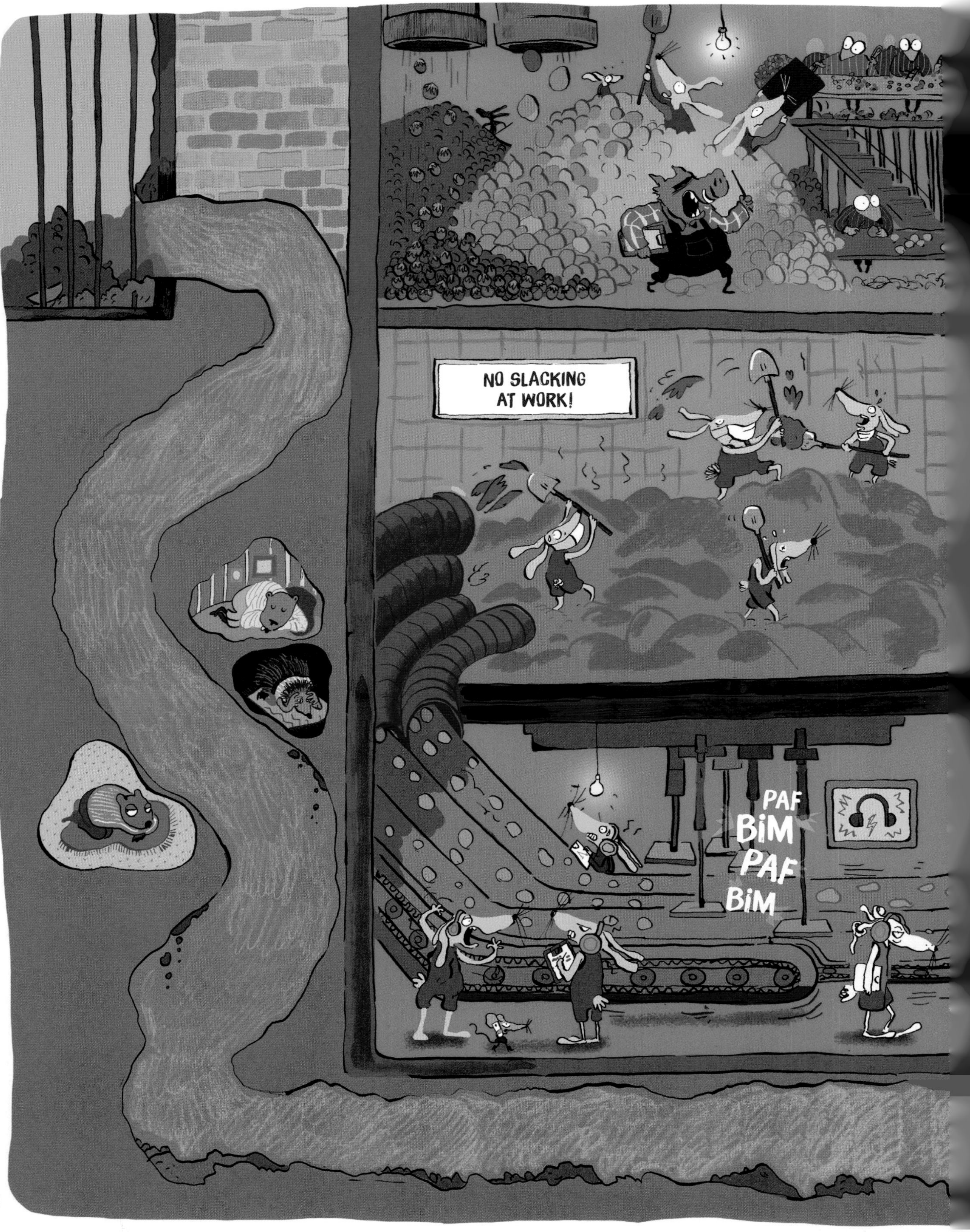
NO SLACKING
AT WORK!
PAF
BIM
PAF
BIM

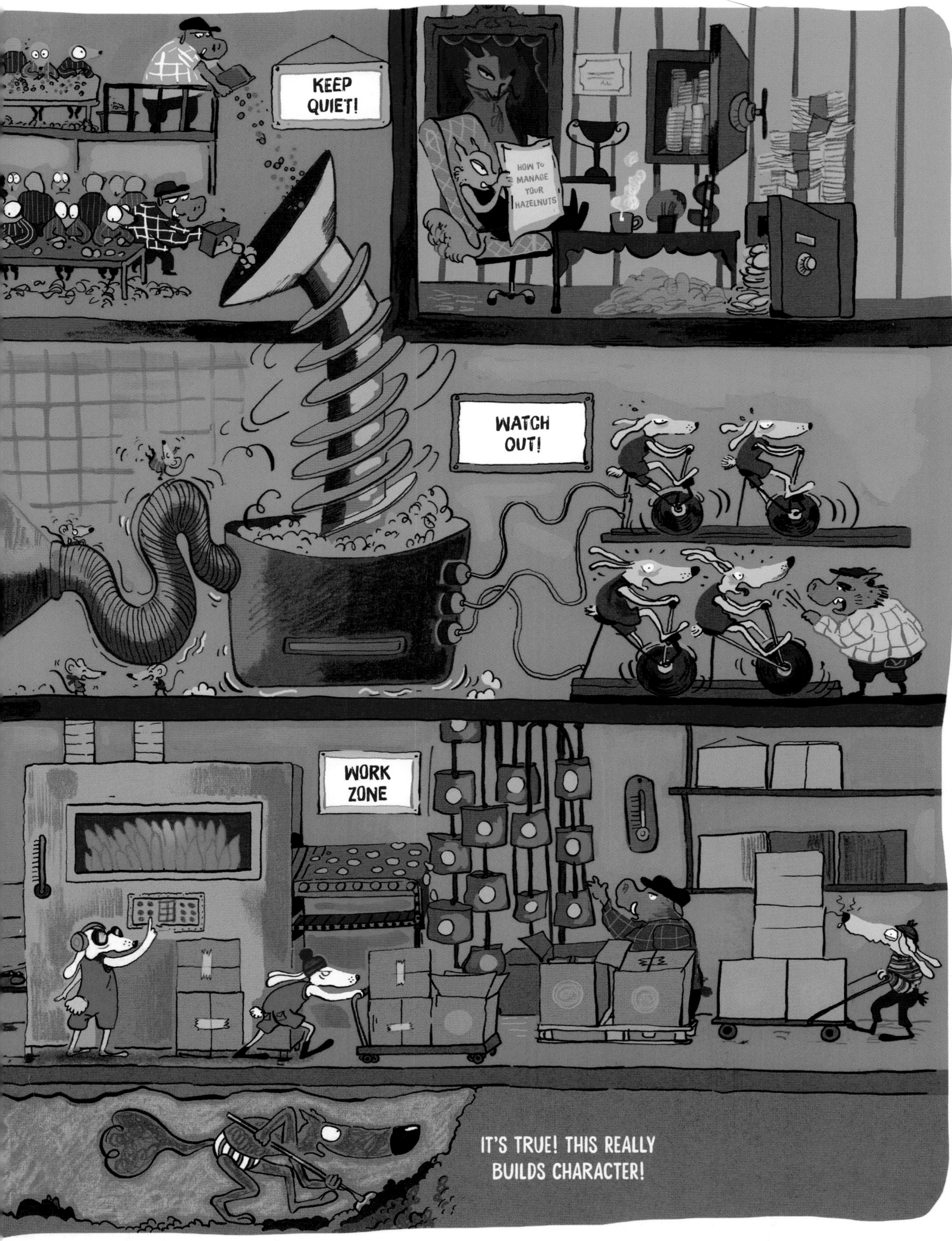
KEEP QUIET!
HOW TO MANAGE YOUR HAZELNUTS
WATCH OUT!
WORK ZONE
IT'S TRUE! THIS REALLY BUILDS CHARACTER!

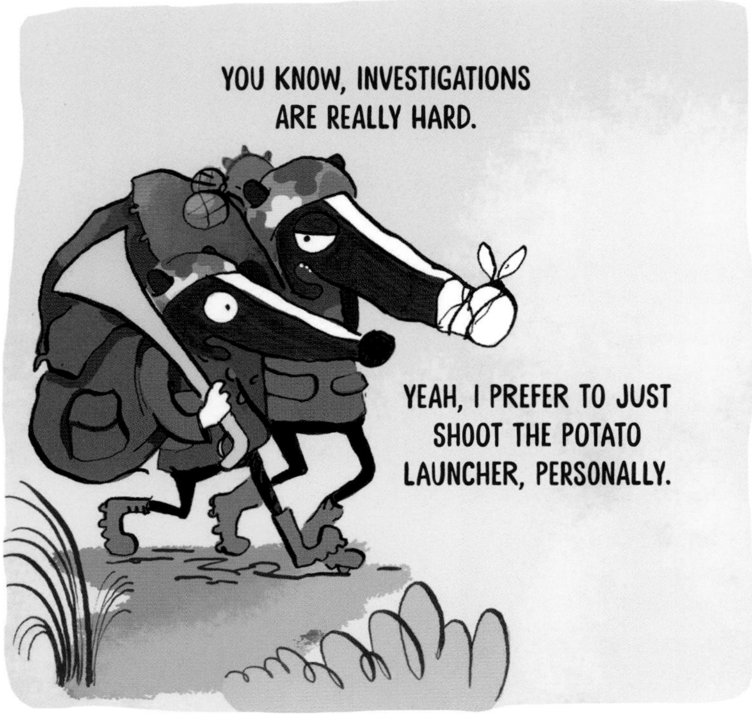
YOU KNOW, INVESTIGATIONS ARE REALLY HARD.
YEAH, I PREFER TO JUST SHOOT THE POTATO LAUNCHER, PERSONALLY.

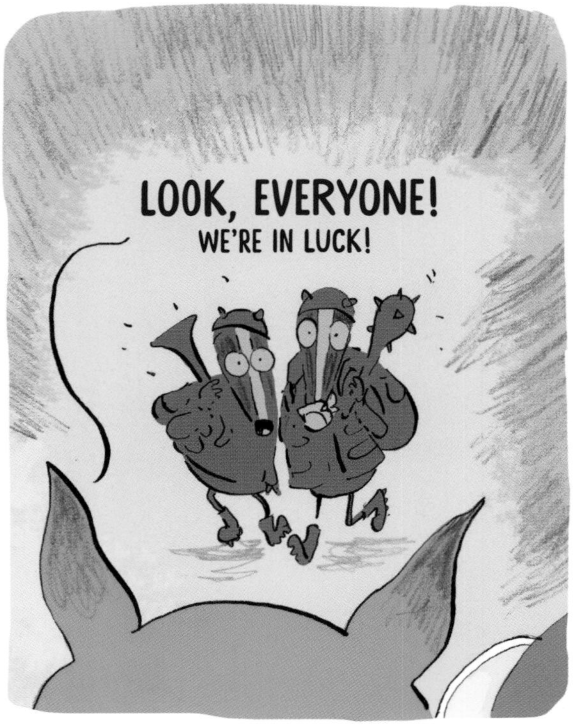
LOOK, EVERYONE! WE'RE IN LUCK!

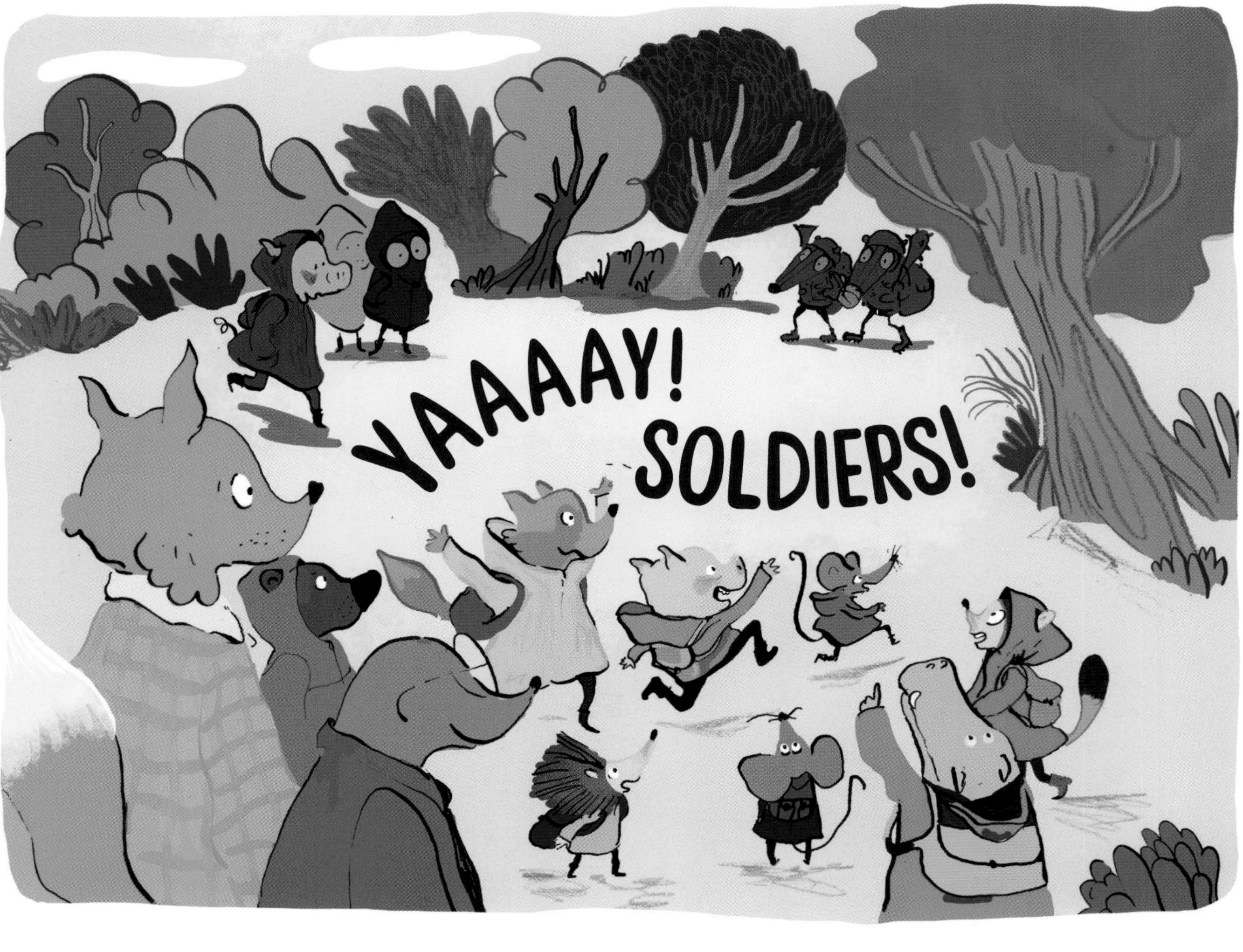
YAAAAY! SOLDIERS!

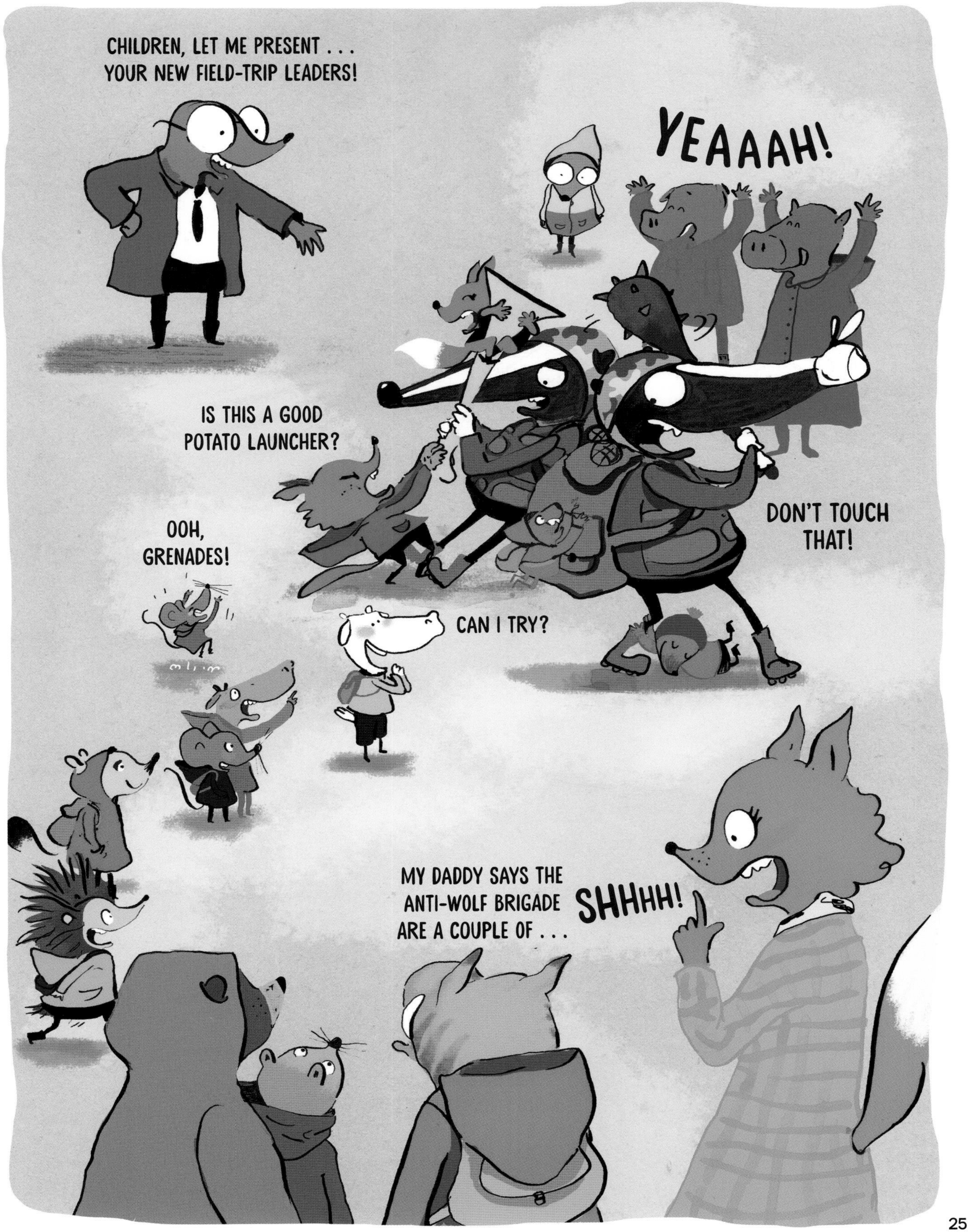

CHILDREN, LET ME PRESENT . . . YOUR NEW FIELD-TRIP LEADERS!
YEAAAH!
IS THIS A GOOD POTATO LAUNCHER?
DON'T TOUCH THAT!
OOH, GRENADES!
CAN I TRY?
MY DADDY SAYS THE ANTI-WOLF BRIGADE ARE A COUPLE OF . . .
SHHHH!

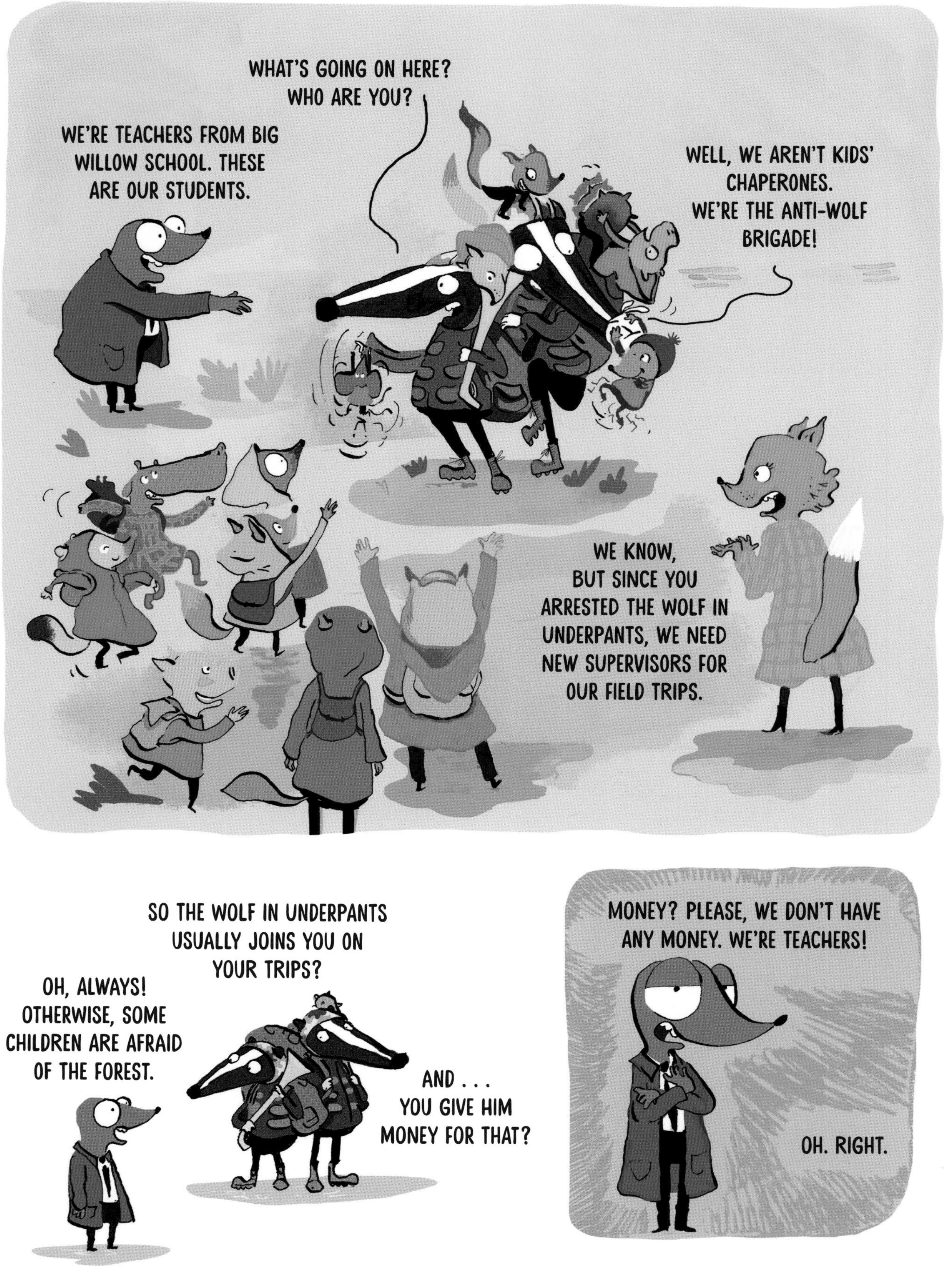
WHAT'S GOING ON HERE? WHO ARE YOU?
WE'RE TEACHERS FROM BIG WILLOW SCHOOL. THESE ARE OUR STUDENTS.
WELL, WE AREN'T KIDS' CHAPERONES. WE'RE THE ANTI-WOLF BRIGADE!
WE KNOW, BUT SINCE YOU ARRESTED THE WOLF IN UNDERPANTS, WE NEED NEW SUPERVISORS FOR OUR FIELD TRIPS.
SO THE WOLF IN UNDERPANTS USUALLY JOINS YOU ON YOUR TRIPS?
OH, ALWAYS! OTHERWISE, SOME CHILDREN ARE AFRAID OF THE FOREST.
AND . . . YOU GIVE HIM MONEY FOR THAT?
MONEY? PLEASE, WE DON'T HAVE ANY MONEY. WE'RE TEACHERS!
OH. RIGHT.

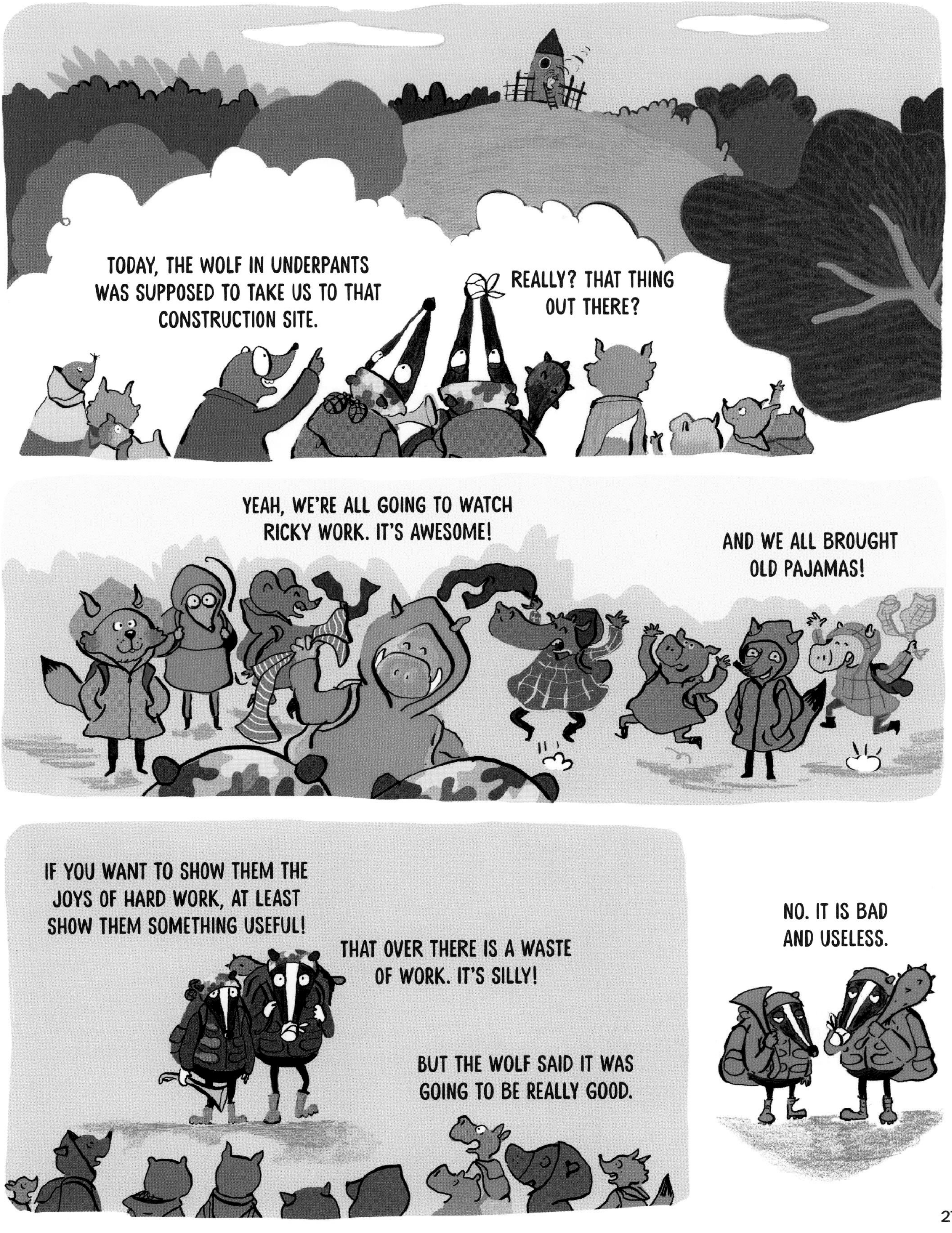
TODAY, THE WOLF IN UNDERPANTS WAS SUPPOSED TO TAKE US TO THAT CONSTRUCTION SITE.
REALLY? THAT THING OUT THERE?
YEAH, WE'RE ALL GOING TO WATCH RICKY WORK. IT'S AWESOME!
AND WE ALL BROUGHT OLD PAJAMAS!
IF YOU WANT TO SHOW THEM THE JOYS OF HARD WORK, AT LEAST SHOW THEM SOMETHING USEFUL!
THAT OVER THERE IS A WASTE OF WORK. IT'S SILLY!
BUT THE WOLF SAID IT WAS GOING TO BE REALLY GOOD.
NO. IT IS BAD AND USELESS.

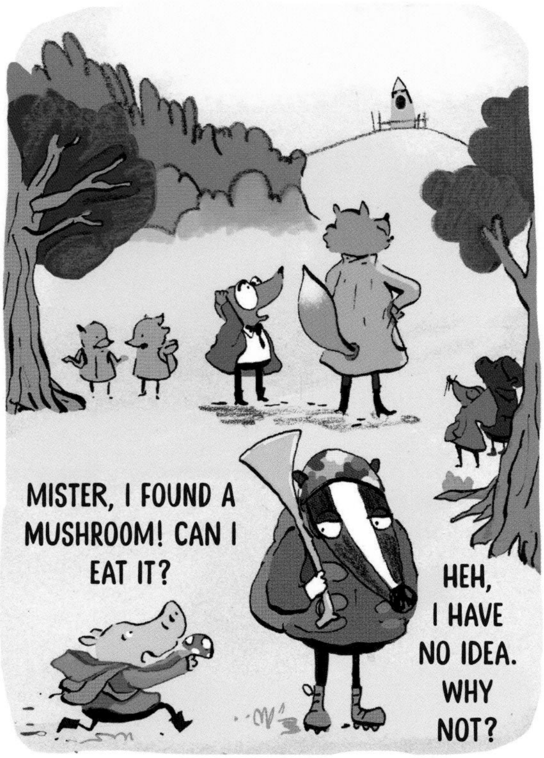
MISTER, I FOUND A MUSHROOM! CAN I EAT IT?
HEH, I HAVE NO IDEA. WHY NOT?

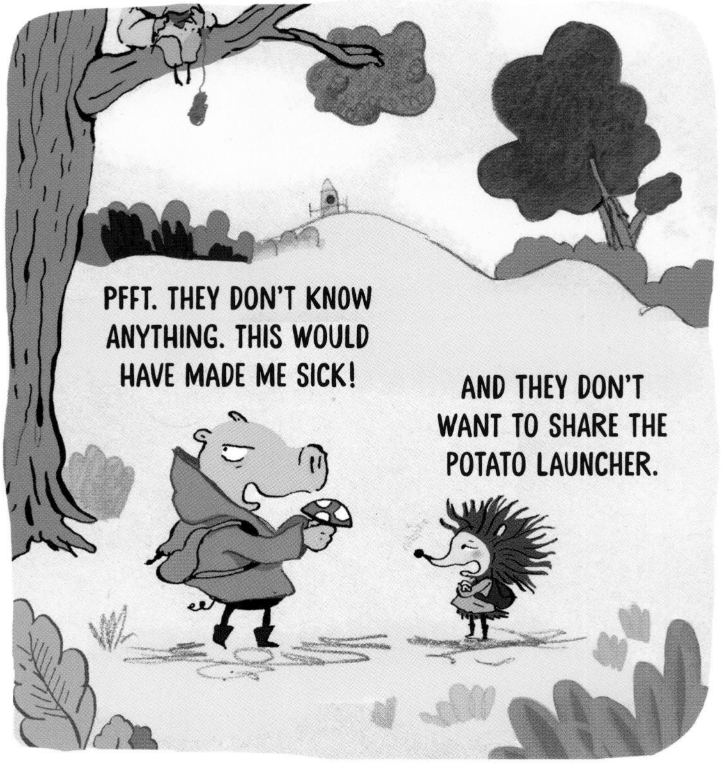
PFFT. THEY DON'T KNOW ANYTHING. THIS WOULD HAVE MADE ME SICK!
AND THEY DON'T WANT TO SHARE THE POTATO LAUNCHER.

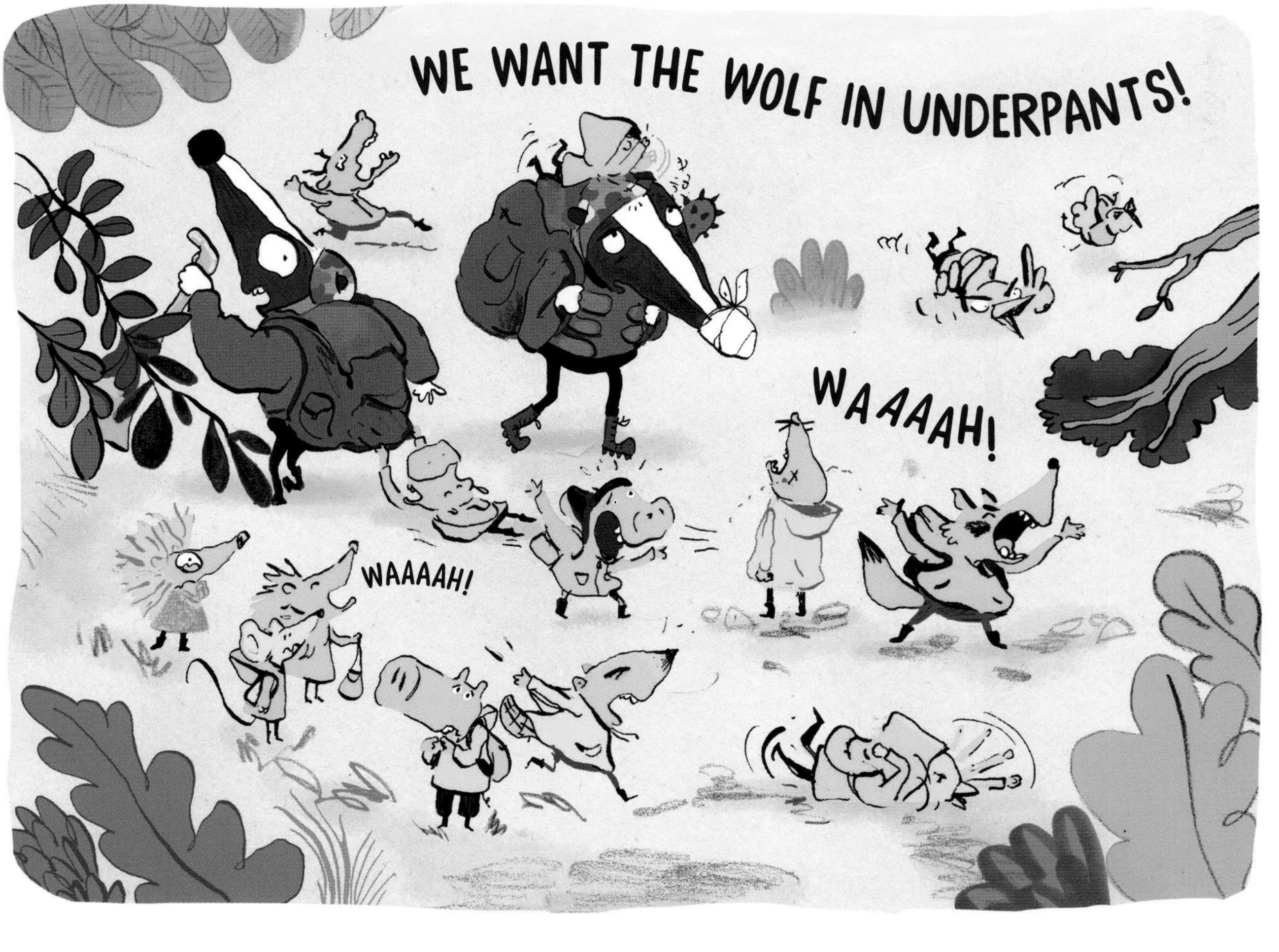
WE WANT THE WOLF IN UNDERPANTS!
WAAAAH!
WAAAAH!

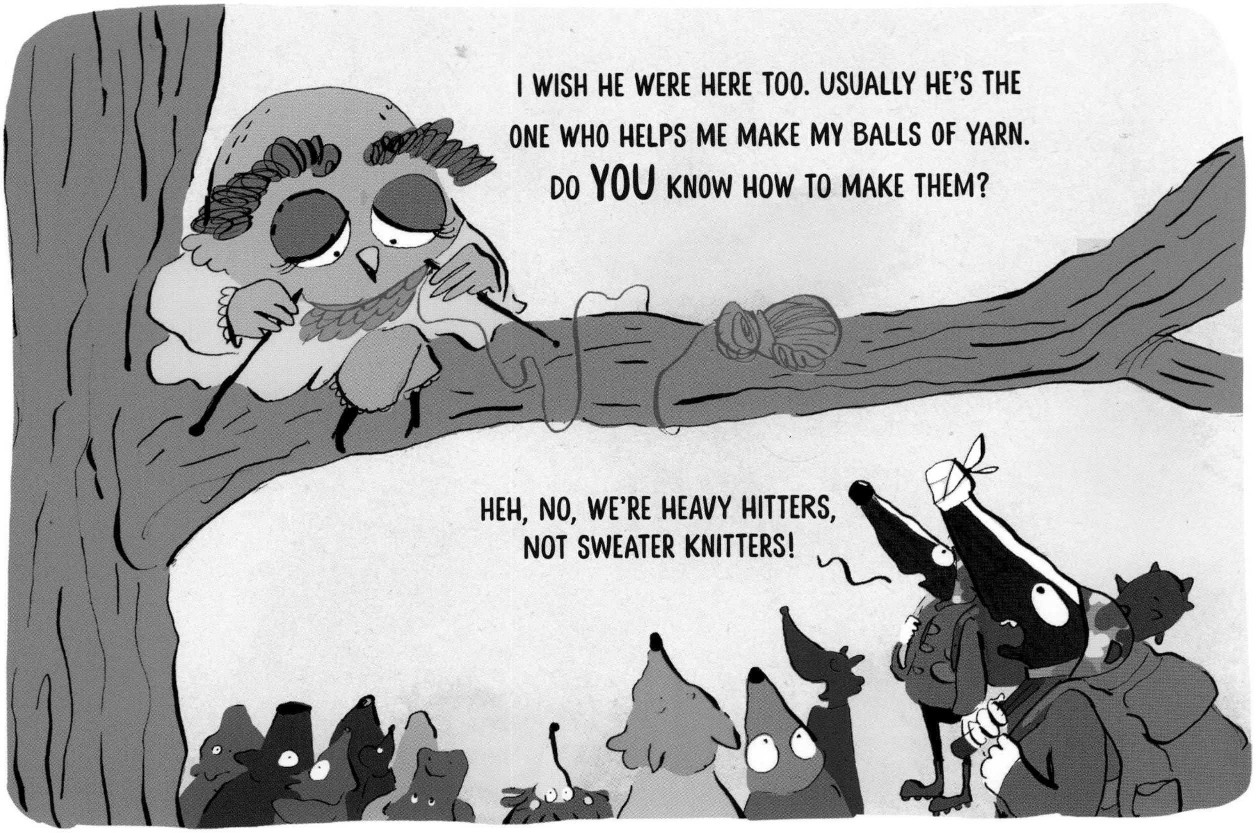
I WISH HE WERE HERE TOO. USUALLY HE'S THE ONE WHO HELPS ME MAKE MY BALLS OF YARN. DO YOU KNOW HOW TO MAKE THEM?
HEH, NO, WE'RE HEAVY HITTERS, NOT SWEATER KNITTERS!

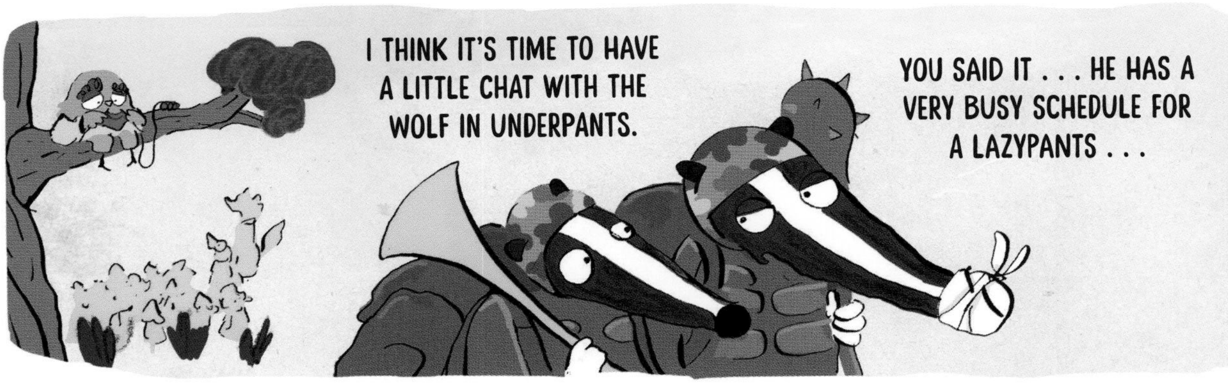
I THINK IT'S TIME TO HAVE A LITTLE CHAT WITH THE WOLF IN UNDERPANTS.
YOU SAID IT . . . HE HAS A VERY BUSY SCHEDULE FOR A LAZYPANTS . . .

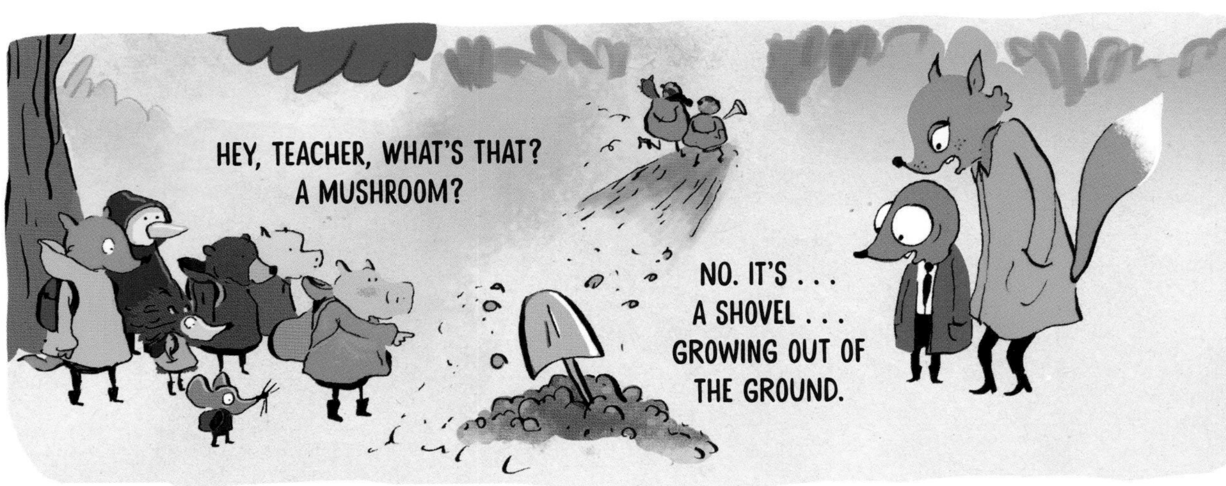
HEY, TEACHER, WHAT'S THAT? A MUSHROOM?
NO. IT'S . . . A SHOVEL . . . GROWING OUT OF THE GROUND.

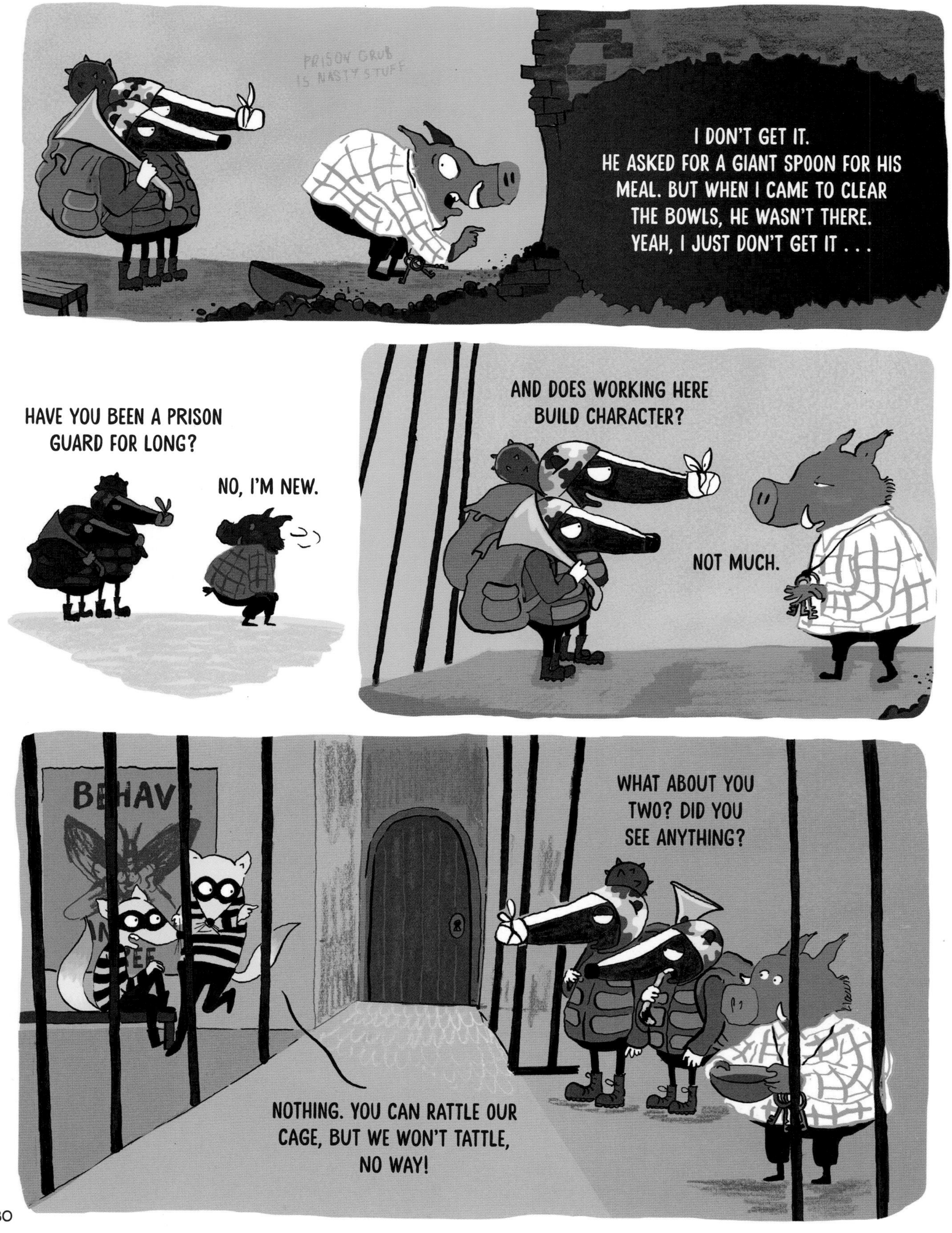
PRISON GRUB IS NASTY STUFF
I DON'T GET IT.
HE ASKED FOR A GIANT SPOON FOR HIS MEAL. BUT WHEN I CAME TO CLEAR THE BOWLS, HE WASN'T THERE.
YEAH, I JUST DON'T GET IT . . .
HAVE YOU BEEN A PRISON GUARD FOR LONG?
NO, I'M NEW.
AND DOES WORKING HERE BUILD CHARACTER?
NOT MUCH.
WHAT ABOUT YOU TWO? DID YOU SEE ANYTHING?
NOTHING. YOU CAN RATTLE OUR CAGE, BUT WE WON'T TATTLE, NO WAY!

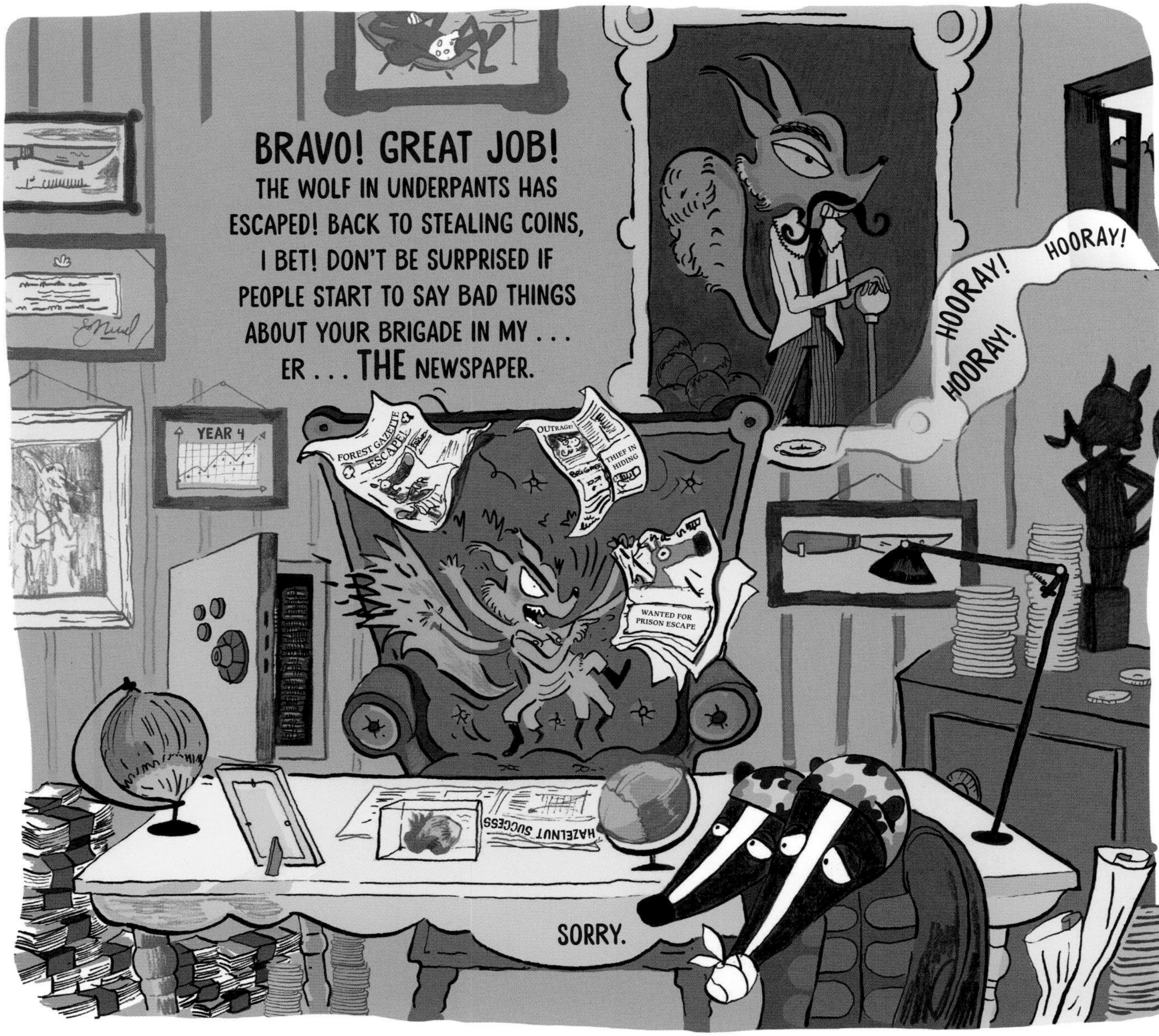
BRAVO! GREAT JOB! THE WOLF IN UNDERPANTS HAS ESCAPED! BACK TO STEALING COINS, I BET! DON'T BE SURPRISED IF PEOPLE START TO SAY BAD THINGS ABOUT YOUR BRIGADE IN MY . . . ER . . . THE NEWSPAPER.
HOORAY! HOORAY! HOORAY!
YEAR 4
FOREST GAZETTE ESCAPE!
OUTRAGE!
THIEF IN HIDING
WANTED FOR PRISON ESCAPE
HAZELNUT SUCCESS
SORRY.

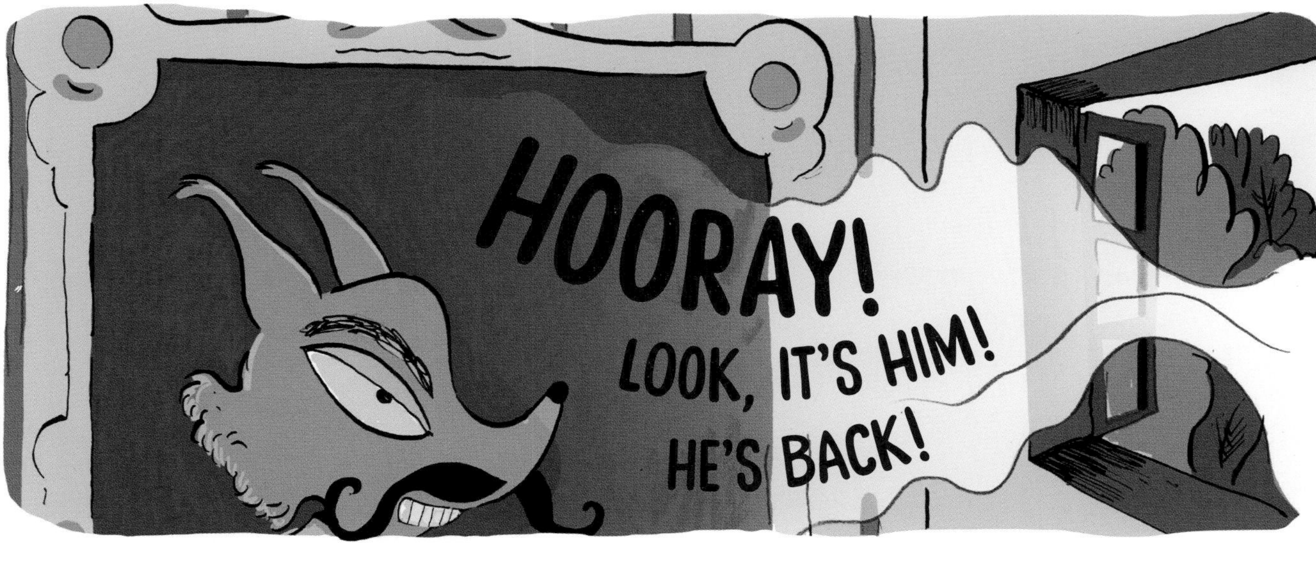
HOORAY!
LOOK, IT'S HIM!
HE'S BACK!

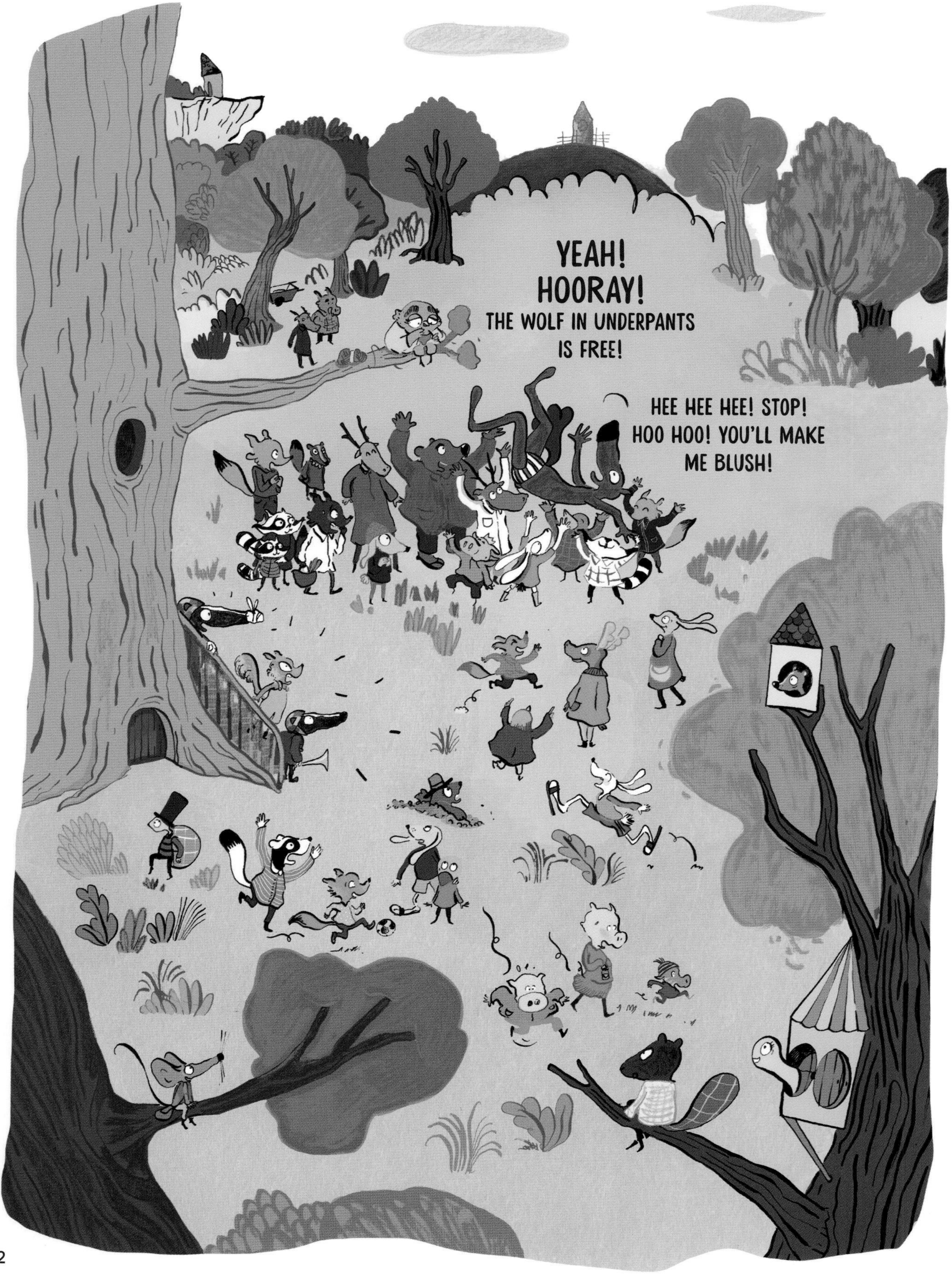
YEAH!
HOORAY!
THE WOLF IN UNDERPANTS
IS FREE!
HEE HEE HEE! STOP!
HOO HOO! YOU'LL MAKE
ME BLUSH!

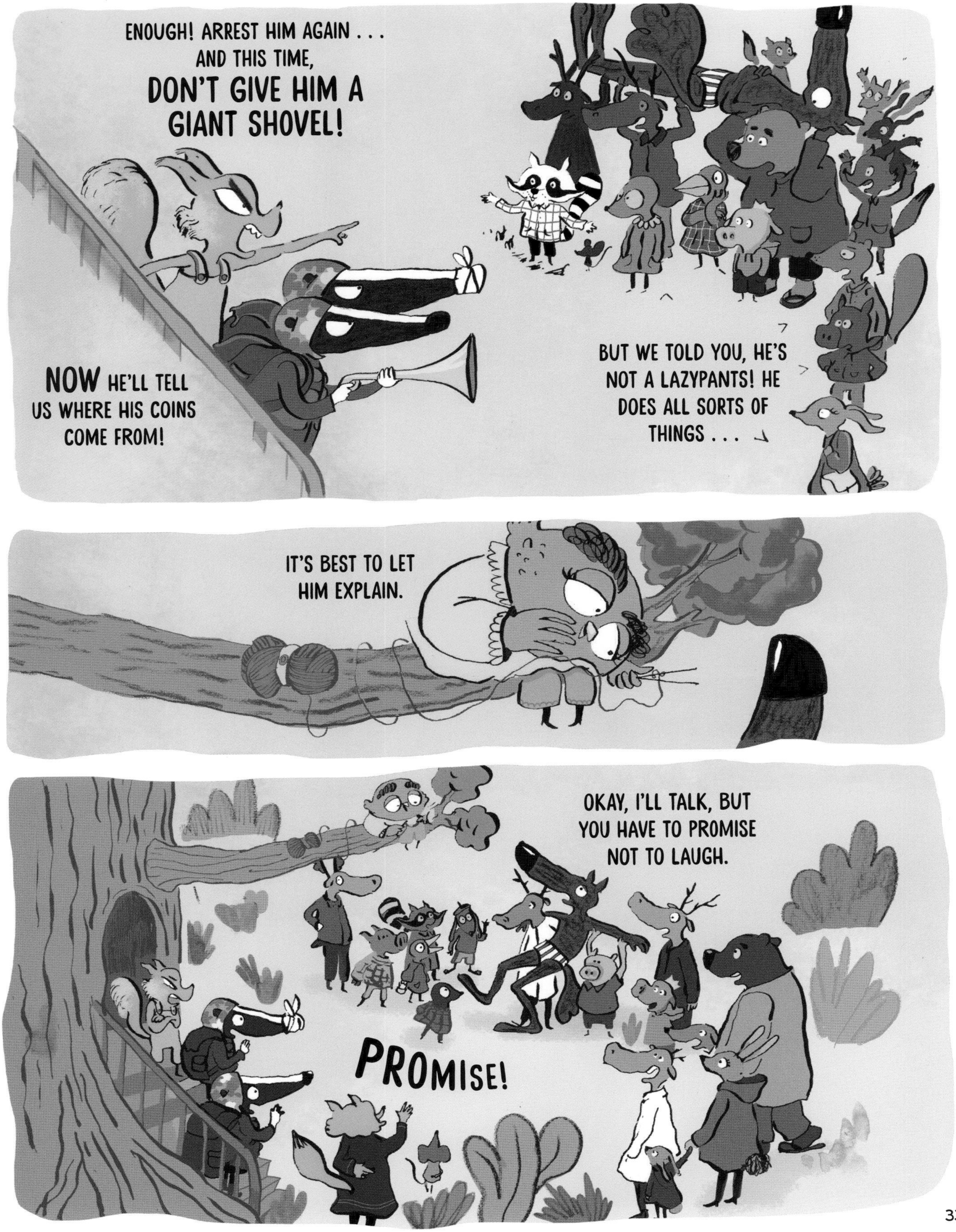
ENOUGH! ARREST HIM AGAIN . . . AND THIS TIME, DON'T GIVE HIM A GIANT SHOVEL!
NOW HE'LL TELL US WHERE HIS COINS COME FROM!
BUT WE TOLD YOU, HE'S NOT A LAZYPANTS! HE DOES ALL SORTS OF THINGS . . .
IT'S BEST TO LET HIM EXPLAIN.
OKAY, I'LL TALK, BUT YOU HAVE TO PROMISE NOT TO LAUGH.
PROMISE!

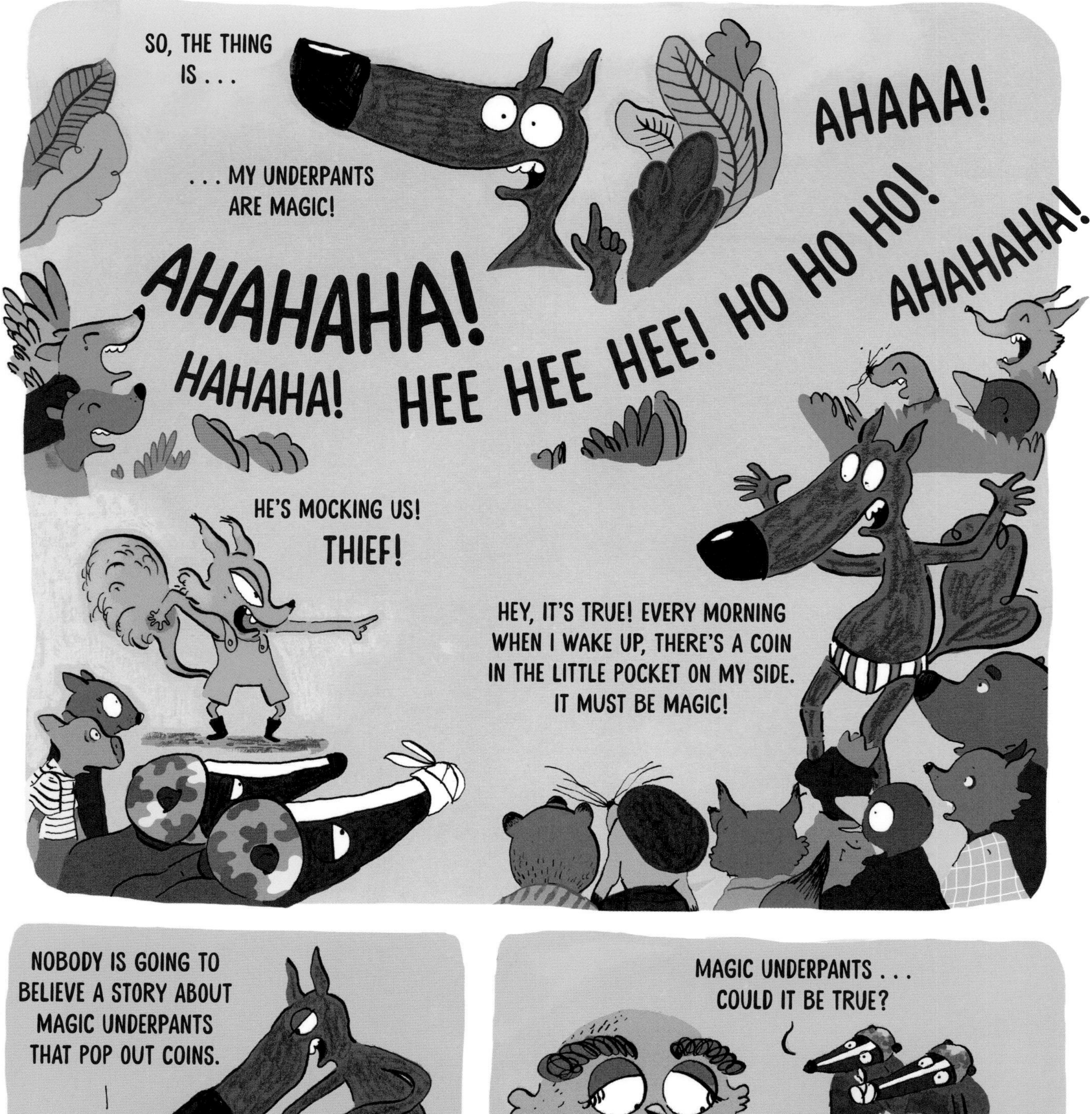
SO, THE THING IS . . .
. . . MY UNDERPANTS ARE MAGIC!
AHAAA!
AHAHAHA!
HAHAHA!
HEE HEE HEE! HO HO HO!
AHAHAHA!
HE'S MOCKING US!
THIEF!
HEY, IT'S TRUE! EVERY MORNING WHEN I WAKE UP, THERE'S A COIN IN THE LITTLE POCKET ON MY SIDE. IT MUST BE MAGIC!

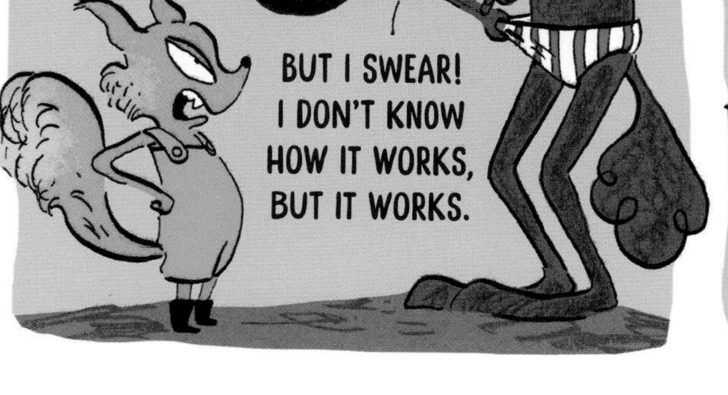
NOBODY IS GOING TO BELIEVE A STORY ABOUT MAGIC UNDERPANTS THAT POP OUT COINS.
BUT I SWEAR! I DON'T KNOW HOW IT WORKS, BUT IT WORKS.

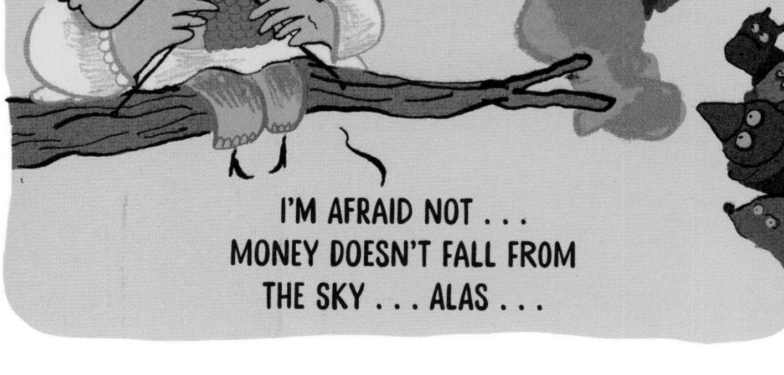
MAGIC UNDERPANTS . . . COULD IT BE TRUE?
I'M AFRAID NOT . . . MONEY DOESN'T FALL FROM THE SKY . . . ALAS . . .

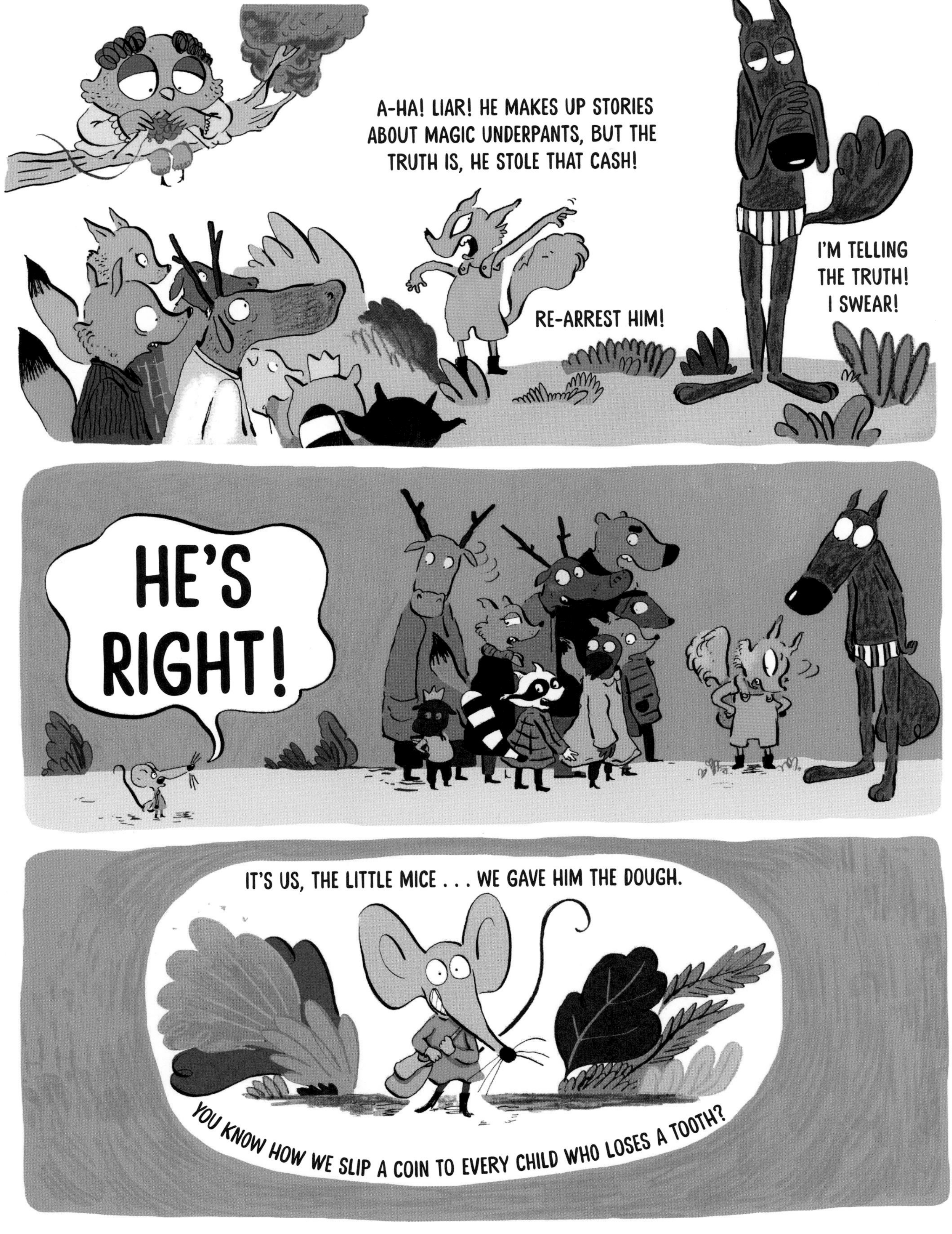
A-HA! LIAR! HE MAKES UP STORIES ABOUT MAGIC UNDERPANTS, BUT THE TRUTH IS, HE STOLE THAT CASH!
RE-ARREST HIM!
I'M TELLING THE TRUTH! I SWEAR!
HE'S RIGHT!
IT'S US, THE LITTLE MICE . . . WE GAVE HIM THE DOUGH.
YOU KNOW HOW WE SLIP A COIN TO EVERY CHILD WHO LOSES A TOOTH?

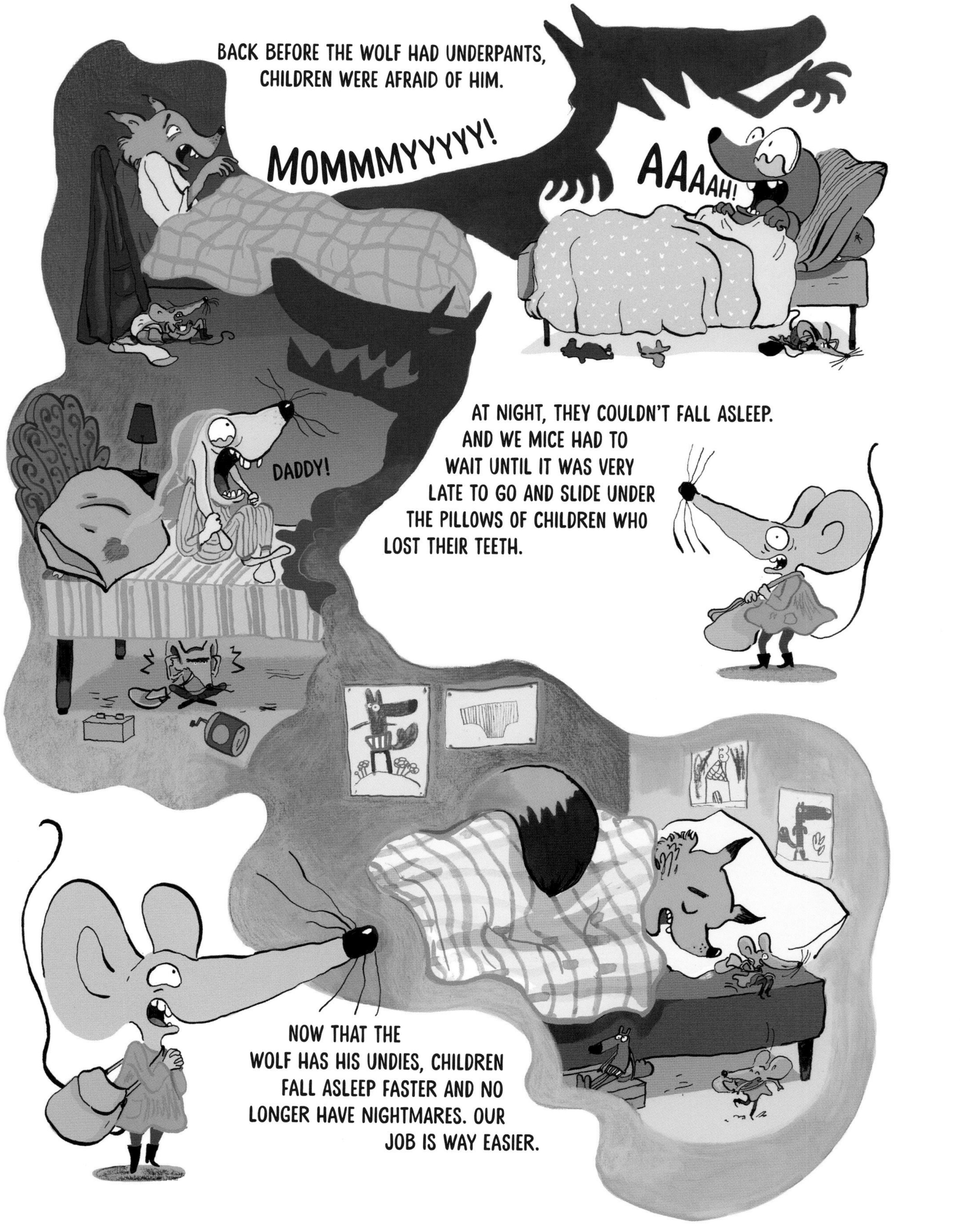
BACK BEFORE THE WOLF HAD UNDERPANTS, CHILDREN WERE AFRAID OF HIM.
MOMMMYYYYY!
AAAAAH!
DADDY!
AT NIGHT, THEY COULDN'T FALL ASLEEP. AND WE MICE HAD TO WAIT UNTIL IT WAS VERY LATE TO GO AND SLIDE UNDER THE PILLOWS OF CHILDREN WHO LOST THEIR TEETH.
NOW THAT THE WOLF HAS HIS UNDIES, CHILDREN FALL ASLEEP FASTER AND NO LONGER HAVE NIGHTMARES. OUR JOB IS WAY EASIER.

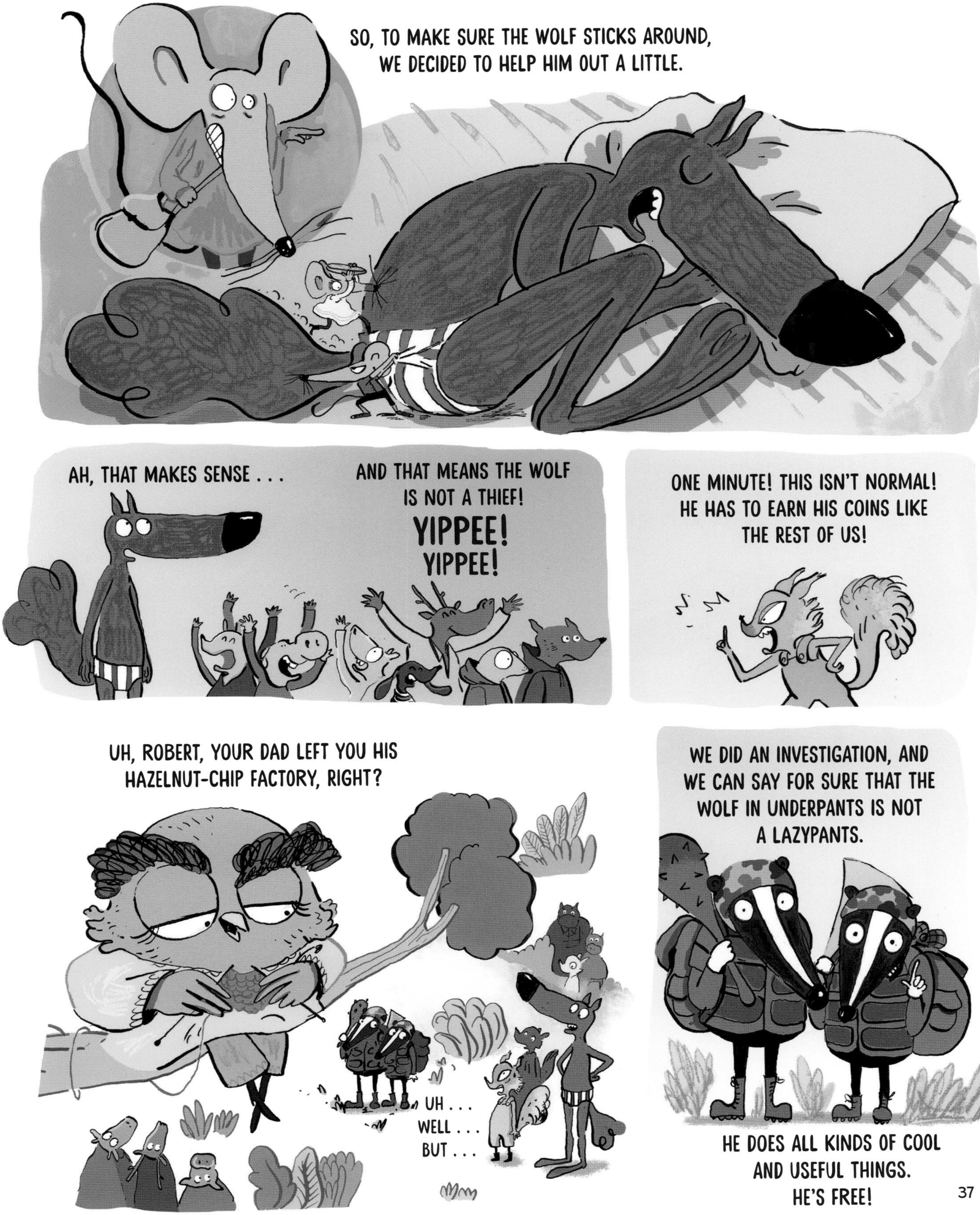
SO, TO MAKE SURE THE WOLF STICKS AROUND, WE DECIDED TO HELP HIM OUT A LITTLE.
AH, THAT MAKES SENSE . . .
AND THAT MEANS THE WOLF IS NOT A THIEF!
YIPPEE! YIPPEE!
ONE MINUTE! THIS ISN'T NORMAL! HE HAS TO EARN HIS COINS LIKE THE REST OF US!
UH, ROBERT, YOUR DAD LEFT YOU HIS HAZELNUT-CHIP FACTORY, RIGHT?
UH . . . WELL . . . BUT . . .
WE DID AN INVESTIGATION, AND WE CAN SAY FOR SURE THAT THE WOLF IN UNDERPANTS IS NOT A LAZYPANTS.
HE DOES ALL KINDS OF COOL AND USEFUL THINGS. HE'S FREE!

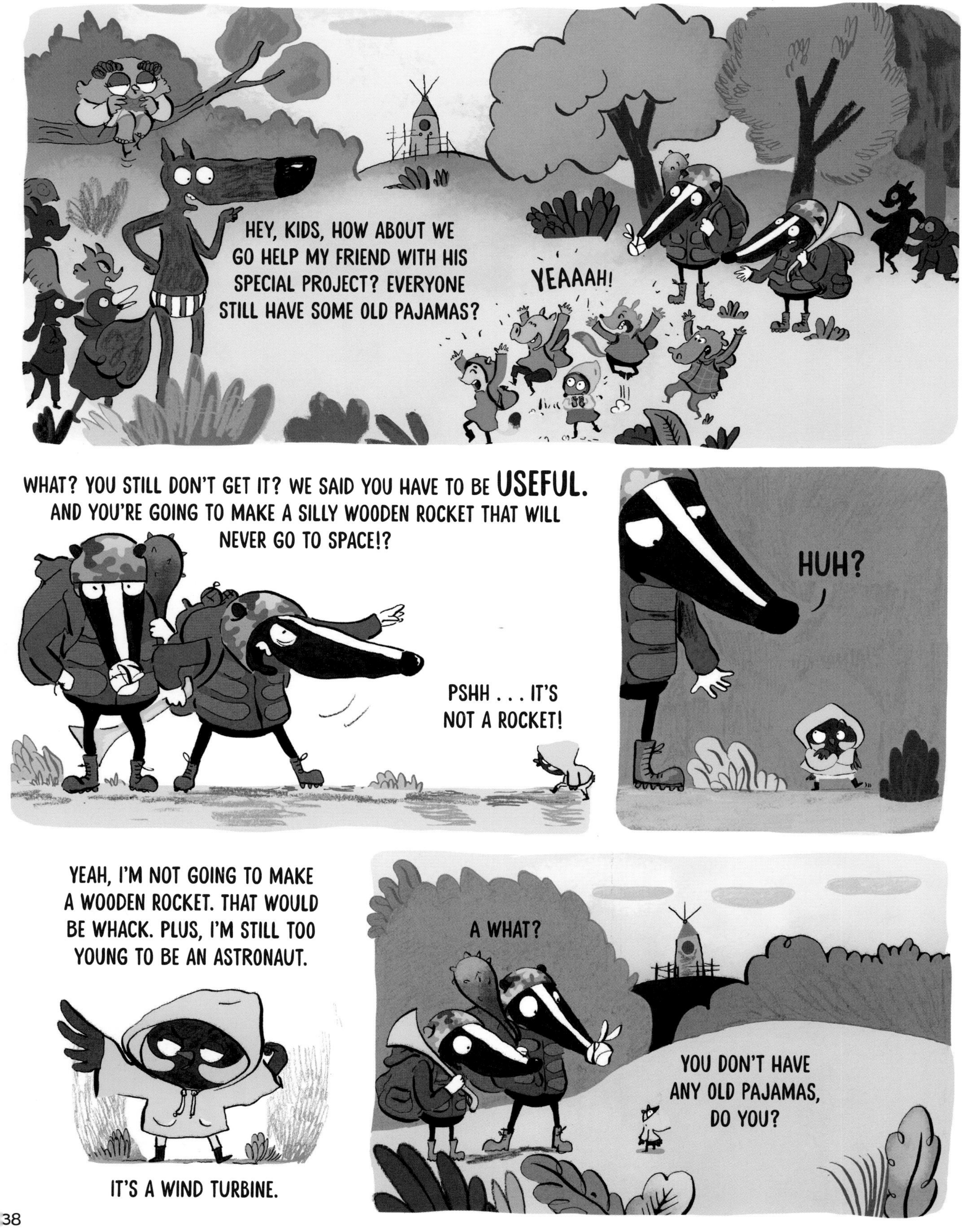
HEY, KIDS, HOW ABOUT WE GO HELP MY FRIEND WITH HIS SPECIAL PROJECT? EVERYONE STILL HAVE SOME OLD PAJAMAS?
YEAAAH!
WHAT? YOU STILL DON'T GET IT? WE SAID YOU HAVE TO BE USEFUL. AND YOU'RE GOING TO MAKE A SILLY WOODEN ROCKET THAT WILL NEVER GO TO SPACE!?
PSHH . . . IT'S NOT A ROCKET!
HUH?
YEAH, I'M NOT GOING TO MAKE A WOODEN ROCKET. THAT WOULD BE WHACK. PLUS, I'M STILL TOO YOUNG TO BE AN ASTRONAUT.
IT'S A WIND TURBINE.
A WHAT?
YOU DON'T HAVE ANY OLD PAJAMAS, DO YOU?

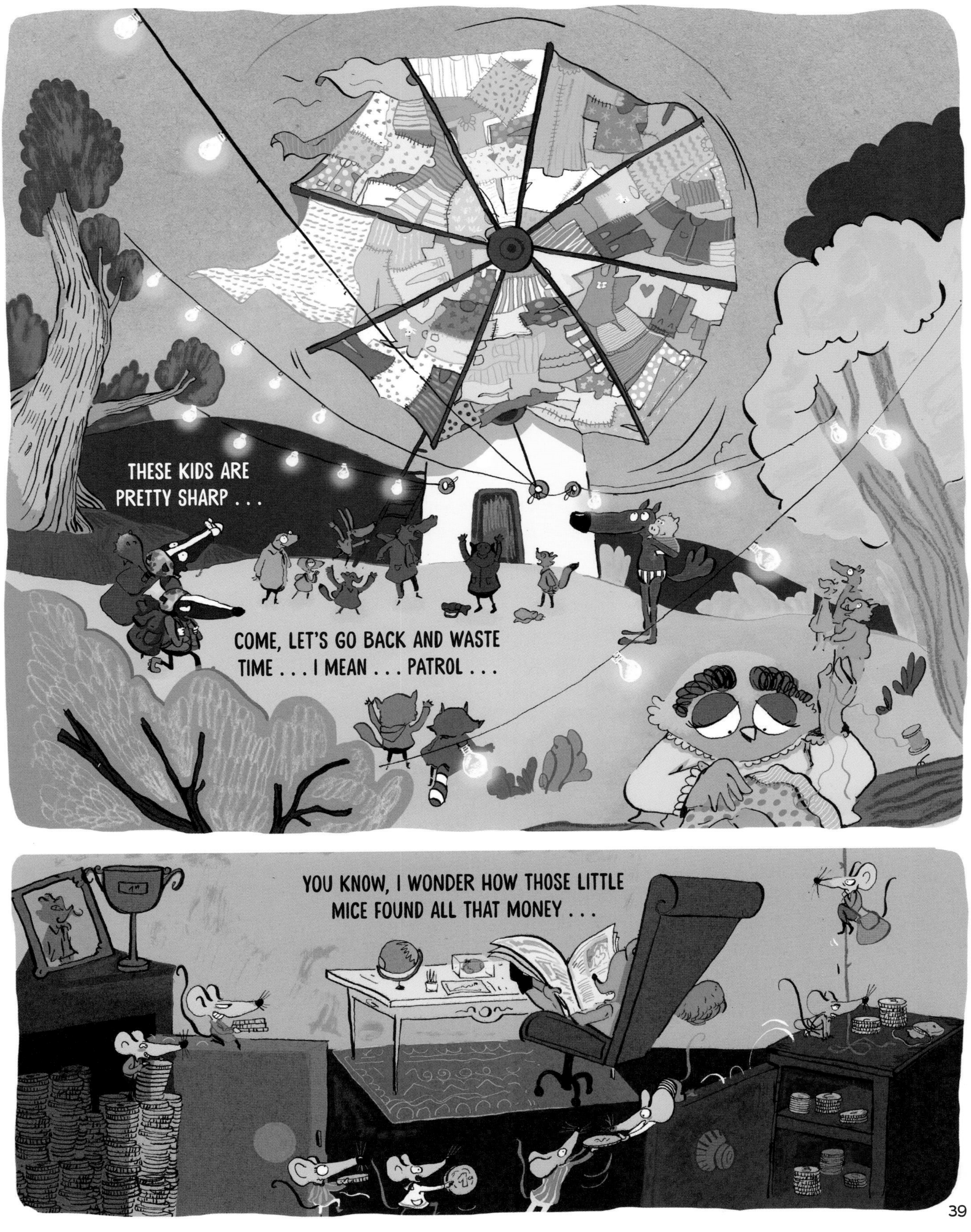
THESE KIDS ARE PRETTY SHARP . . .
COME, LET'S GO BACK AND WASTE TIME . . . I MEAN . . . PATROL . . .
YOU KNOW, I WONDER HOW THOSE LITTLE MICE FOUND ALL THAT MONEY . . .

ABOUT THE CREATORS

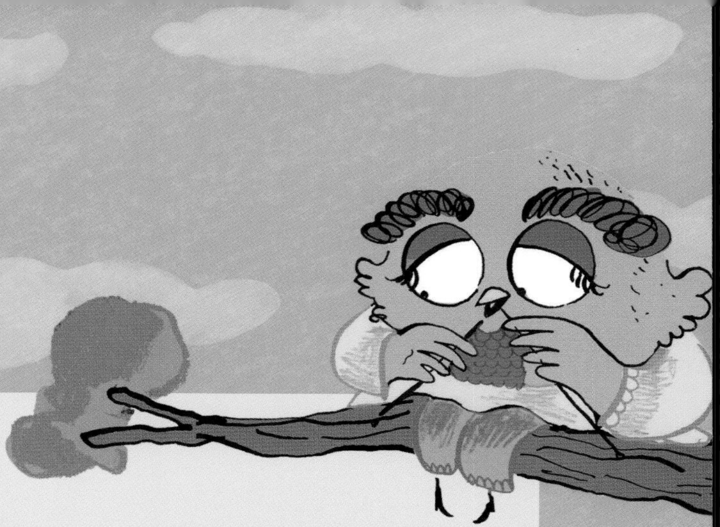

WILFRID LUPANO

Wilfrid Lupano was born in Nantes, in the west of France, and spent most of his childhood in the southwestern city of Pau, France. He spent his childhood reading through his parents' comic book collection and enjoying role-playing games. He studied literature and philosophy, receiving a degree in English, before he began to script comics. He has written numerous graphic novels for French readers, including the series *Les Vieux Fourneaux* (in English, *The Old Geezers*). With this series, Lupano and Paul Cauuet first developed the idea that would become *The Wolf in Underpants*. Lupano once again lives in Pau after spending several years in the city of Toulouse.

MAYANA ITOÏZ

Mayana Itoïz was born in the city of Bayonne, in the southwest of France, and studied at the institut supérieur des arts de Toulouse (School of Fine Arts in Toulouse), where she worked in many different mediums. In addition to being an illustrator and a cartoonist, she has taught art to high school students. She lives in the Pyrenees, near France's mountainous southern border, and splits her time between art, family, and travel.

PAUL CAUUET

Paul Cauuet was born in Toulouse and grew up in a family that encouraged his passion for drawing. He was also a fond reader of classic Franco-Belgian comics such as *Tintin* and *Asterix*. He studied at the University of Toulouse and went on to a career as a cartoonist. Cauuet and Wilfrid Lupano first collaborated on an outer-space comedy series before working together on *Les Vieux Fourneaux* (*The Old Geezers*).

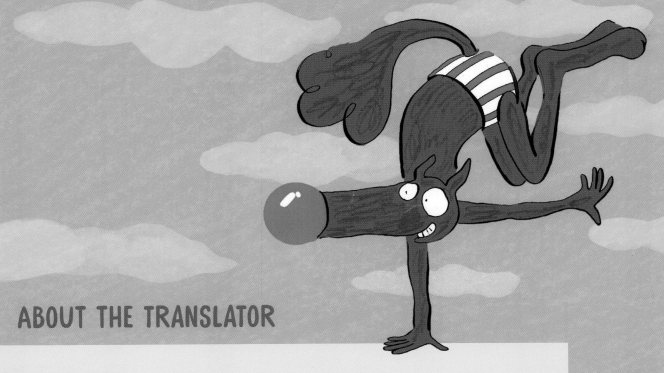

ABOUT THE TRANSLATOR

NATHAN SACKS

Nathan Sacks is a writer, editor, and translator from Ames, Iowa, who lives in Los Angeles. He has written fiction and nonfiction children's books and translated several graphic novels from French to English.

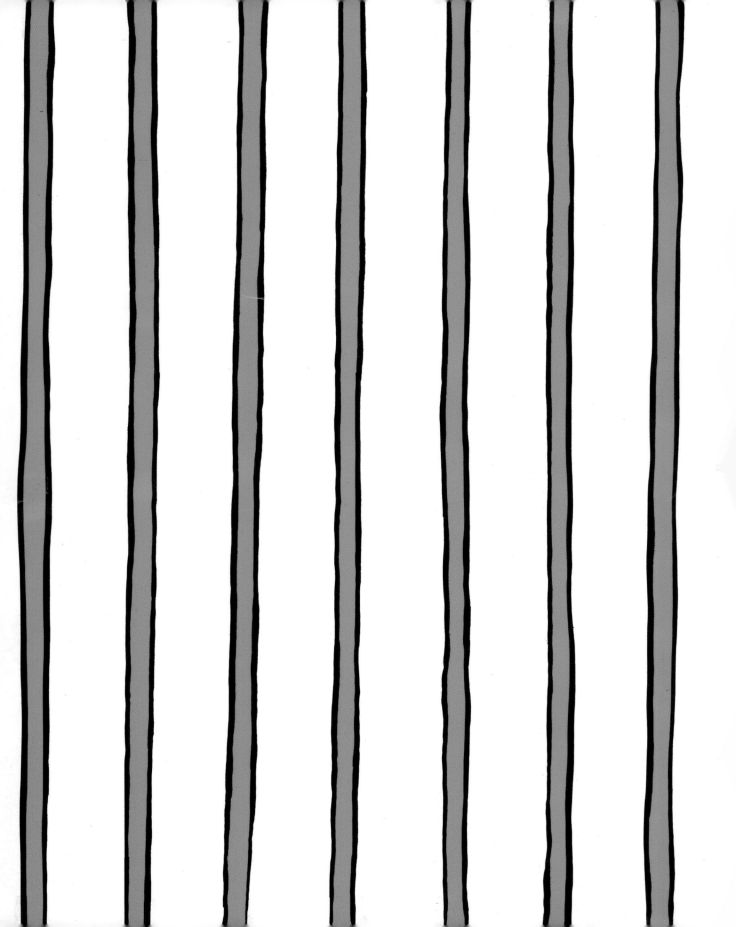